THE
BREWER
of
PRESTON

By Andrea Camilleri

Inspector Montalbano Mysteries

The Shape of Water

The Terracotta Dog

The Snack Thief

Voice of the Violin

Excursion to Tindari

The Scent of the Night

Rounding the Mark

The Patience of the Spider

The Paper Moon

August Heat

The Wings of the Sphinx

The Track of Sand

The Potter's Field

The Age of Doubt

The Dance of the Seagull

Treasure Hunt

Angelica's Smile

Game of Mirrors

Blade of Light

Other novels

Hunting Season

The Brewer of Preston

THE
BREWER
of
PRESTON

Andrea Camilleri

Translated by Stephen Sartarelli

MANTLE

First published 2014 by Penguin Books,
a member of Penguin Group (USA) Inc., New York

This edition published 2016 by Mantle
an imprint of Pan Macmillan
20 New Wharf Road, London N1 9RR
Associated companies throughout the world
www.panmacmillan.com

ISBN 978-1-4472-9218-0

THE
BREWER
of
PRESTON

It was a frightful night

It was a frightful night, downright scary. As a thunderclap more boisterous than the rest rattled the windowpanes, young Gerd Hoffer, not yet ten years old, woke up with a start, realizing at the same time that he needed to go. It was an old story, this pee problem. The doctors' diagnosis was that ever since birth the child had suffered from weak retention—of the kidneys, that is—and that it was therefore natural for him to relieve himself in bed. His father, however—mining engineer Fridolin Hoffer—wouldn't hear of it. He could not resign himself to having brought a waste of a German boy into the world, and thus he believed that what was needed was not medical care but a Kantian education of the will. For this reason, every morning that the good Lord brought upon the earth, he would inspect his son's bed, raising the blanket or sheet, depending on the season, insert an inquisitorial hand, and inevitably find a wet spot, whereupon he would deal the boy a powerful slap on the cheek, which would swell up like a muffin under the effect of brewer's yeast.

This time, to avoid his father's customary morning punishment, Gerd got up in the dark to the light of the thunderbolts and set out on a tentative journey to the privy, heart galloping in fear of the dangers and ambushes lurking in the night. One time a lizard had climbed up his leg, another time he had crushed a cockroach underfoot, making a squishy sound the mere thought of which still turned his stomach.

Reaching the latrine, he rolled his nightshirt up over his belly and began to urinate. Meanwhile he looked out the low window, as he always did, onto Vigàta and its sea, a few miles beyond Montelusa. He would get excited whenever he managed to spot the faint glow of an acetylene lamp on some lost *paranza*. A kind of music would burst forth in his head, a rush of sensations he couldn't express; only a few scattered words would appear and glitter like stars in a black sky. He would start to sweat and, when back in bed, could no longer fall back asleep, tossing and turning until the bedsheets became a sort of hangman's rope around his neck. A number of years later he would become a poet and author, but he did not know this yet.

That night it was different. Between the lightning, the thunder, and the flashes on the horizon, all of which frightened him as much as they fascinated him, he saw a phenomenon he had never seen before. Over Vigàta, the sun or something similar seemed to be rising. This, however, was utterly impossible, since his father had shown him, with Teutonic precision and a wealth of scientific detail, that the first light of day always arrived from the opposite direction—that is, from the great picture window in the dining room.

He looked more carefully; there could no longer be any doubt: a reddish half-moon covered the sky over Vigàta. Against the light, he could actually see the shapes of the most elevated buildings, the ones on the Piano della Lanterna, which loomed over the town.

He knew from painful experience how dangerous it was to wake his father up when he was fast asleep, but he decided that this time the circumstances called for it. Because there were only two possibilities: either the earth, having grown weary of always turning in the same direction, had changed course (the very idea of it made his head spin with excitement, born as he was a poet and author); or his father had, for once, fallen short of his sovereign infallibility (and this second prospect made his head spin even more, born as he was a son). He headed towards his father's room, happy that his mother wasn't there—she was in Tübingen to help out Grandma Wilhelmina—and, the moment he entered, he was overwhelmed by the cataclysmic snoring of the engineer, a great hulk of a man measuring almost six foot six and weighing nearly nineteen stone, with red crew-cut hair and a big handlebar mustache, also red. The boy touched the noisy mass and withdrew his hand at once, as if he had burnt himself.

"Eh?" said his father, eyes immediately wide open, as he was a light sleeper.

"*Vater*," Gerd muttered. "Father."

"*Was ist denn?* What's wrong?" asked the engineer, striking a match and lighting the lamp on his nightstand.

"The night's making light over Vigàta."

"Light? What light? Morning light?"

"Yes, *Vater*."

Without saying another word, the engineer gestured to his son to draw near, and as soon as the boy was within reach, he dealt him a terrific slap.

The child staggered, brought a hand to his cheek, but only hardened in his resolve. He repeated:

"That's right, *Vater*, it's making morning light over Vigàta."

"Ko at vunce to your room!" the engineer ordered him. Never would he let his son's eyes—which he presumed to be innocent—see him get out of bed in his nightshirt.

Gerd obeyed. Something strange must be happening, the engineer thought as he put on a dressing gown and headed to the bathroom. A single glance was more than enough to convince him that, never mind the morning light, a fire, and a big one, had broken out in Vigàta. If he listened hard, he could even hear a church bell ringing frantically.

"*Mein Gott!*" said the engineer, almost breathless. Then, barely containing his urge to shout for joy, he frantically got dressed, opened the main drawer of his desk, withdrew a big golden trumpet equipped with a cordon to sling it over the shoulder, and raced out of the house without bothering to shut the door behind him.

∿∿∿

Once in the street, he let out a long whinny of contentment and began to run. Thanks to the fire, he would have his first chance to test the ingenious fire-extinguishing device he was planning to patent, which he had built from his own designs over long months of passionate labor during off-hours from the mine. It was a broad cart without side panels, and a thick slab of iron nailed onto its flat bed. Tightly screwed onto this slab was a sort of gigantic copper alembic, which was connected to another, smaller alembic, beneath which a cast-iron compartment, open on top, served as a boiler. The little alembic, when filled with water and heated by the fire below, produced, in keeping with Papin's astonishing discovery, the pressure needed to drive the cold water held in the larger alembic forcefully outward. Hitched to the big cart was a smaller one that carried firewood and two ladders that could be coupled together. The whole thing was drawn by four horses; a team of six volunteer firefighters would take up standing positions on either side of the large cart. During training sessions and rehearsals, the machine had always produced good results.

Arriving at the top of the street that sliced through the former Arab quarter now inhabited by miners and *zolfatari*, Fridolin Hoffer took a deep breath and sounded a shrill blast on his trumpet. He walked all the way down the long street, his broad barrel chest sore from the force with which he repeatedly blew into the trumpet. When he reached the end, he did an abrupt about-face and began to walk back up the street, resuming his blowing.

The effects of his midnight horn blowing were immediate. The men of his team, forewarned of the meaning of an impromptu nighttime reveille to the blasts of a trumpet, started dressing in haste after reassuring their trembling wives and bawling children. Then one of them ran to the storehouse where the machine was kept while the coachman took care of attaching the horses, and a third and a fourth lit the fire under the small alembic.

The other inhabitants of the populous neighborhood, unaware of anything but duly terrorized by the blasts of the trumpet, which sounded like the heralds of the Last Judgment, barricaded themselves as best they could behind doors and windows in a tumult of shouts, cries, yells, sobs, prayers, ejaculations, and curses. Suddenly awakened, Signora Nunziata Lo Monaco, ninety-three years old, became immediately convinced that the riots of '48 had returned and panicked, froze, and fell backwards as stiff as a broomstick relegated to its dusty corner. Her family found her dead the following morning and laid the blame on her heart and her age, and certainly not on the German's ultrahigh C.

The team of firefighters, meanwhile, having completed their preparations, gathered closely around the engineer. They were nervous and excited about the great opportunity before them. The engineer looked them in the eye one by one, then raised an arm and gave the signal to start. In a flash they climbed aboard and headed off to Vigàta at a gallop. Every few minutes Hoffer gave a blast of the trumpet slung over his shoulder, perhaps to warn any rabbits or dogs that might find themselves in his path, since there certainly were no people about at that hour on a night of such dreadful weather.

                        ⋙

For Gerd, too, who'd been left alone at home, it was a strange night. Hearing his father leave, he got up out of bed, went and locked the front door, and lit all the lamps in the house, one after the other, until he was in a sea of light. Then he sat down in front of the mirror in his mother's bedroom. (The engineer and his wife slept in separate rooms, which was the biggest scandal in town and considered scarcely Christian, but in any case nobody really knew what religion the German and his wife belonged to.) He took off his nightshirt and, sitting there naked, began staring at himself. Then he went into his father's study, grabbed a ruler from the desktop, and returned to the mirror, which was a full-length glass. Taking in hand the thing between his legs (dick? peter? cock?

peepee?), he held it along the ruler. Repeating the action several times, he remained unsatisfied with the measurement, despite having pulled on the skin so hard that it hurt. He laid down the ruler and, discouraged, went back to bed. Closing his eyes, he began to address a long and detailed prayer to God, asking Him, by apposite miracle, to make his thing like that of his classmate Sarino Guastella, who was as tall as he, weighed the same as he, but was inexplicably four times longer and thicker down there than he was.

〰

When they got to the Piano della Lanterna, below which lay the town of Vigàta, the engineer and his men realized, to their consternation, that the fire was no joking matter. There were at least two large buildings in flames. As they stood there watching, and the engineer contemplated which side of the hill they should descend with their machine in order to attack the flames most quickly, they saw, by the dancing light of the blaze, a man walking as if lost in thought, though swaying from time to time. His clothes were burnt and his hair stood straight up, either from fear or by choice of style, it wasn't clear which. He was holding his hands over his head, as if in surrender. They stopped him, having had to call to him twice, as the man seemed not to have heard them.

"Vat is happenink?" asked the engineer.

"Where?" the man asked back in a polite voice.

"Vat you mean, vere? In Figata, vat is happenink?"

"In Vigàta?"

"Yes," they all said in a sort of chorus.

"There seems to be a fire," said the man, looking down at the town as if to confirm.

"But how come it happent? You know?"

The man lowered his arms, put them behind his back, and looked down at his shoes.

"You don't know?" he asked.

"No, ve don't know."

"I see. Apparently the soprano, at a certain point, hit a wrong note."

Having said this, the man resumed walking, putting his hands again over his head.

"What the hell is the soprano?" asked Tano Alletto, the coachman.

"She's a voman who sinks," Hoffer explained, rousing himself from his astonishment.

A spectre is haunting the musicians of Europe

"A spectre is haunting the musicians of Europe!" Cavaliere Mistretta declared in a loud voice, slamming his hand down hard on the table. It was clear to all present that by "musicians" he meant musical composers. The cavaliere dealt in fava beans and was not very fond of reading, but occasionally, when speaking, he liked to indulge in apocalyptic imagery.

The yell and the crash made the members of the Family and Progress Social Club of Vigàta, already nervous after more than three hours of intense discussion, jump in their seats.

Giosuè Zito, the veteran agronomist, had a very different reaction. Having dozed off some fifteen minutes earlier because he'd been up all night with a terrible toothache, he woke with a start after hearing, in his half sleep, only the word "spectre," then eased himself nimbly out of his chair, knelt on the ground, made the sign of the cross, and started reciting the Credo. Everyone in town knew that three years earlier, when asleep in his country house, the agronomist had been scared out of his wits by a ghost, a spectre that had chased him from room to room amidst a great racket of chains and harrowing laments straight out of hell. After finishing his prayer, Giosuè Zito stood up, still pale as a corpse, turned towards the cavaliere, and said in a trembling voice:

"Don't you ever dare make any mention, Godless man that you are, of spectres or ghosts in my presence! Is that clear, you Calabrian mule? I know how terrifying a ghost can be!"

"You, my friend, don't know a bloody thing."

"How dare you say that?"

"I say it because I can," said Cavaliere Mistretta, annoyed.

"Explain yourself."

"Every last person in town knows that on that famous night, which you've been endlessly telling and retelling us about, boring everyone to death, on that night, I say, you were attacked not by a ghost, but by your scallywag of a brother Giacomino, who dressed himself up in a sheet because he wanted to drive you mad and cheat you out of your share of your father's inheritance."

"What do you mean?"

"What do I mean? I mean there was no ghost. It was your brother Giacomino monkeying around!"

"But I got scared just the same. It had the very same effect on me as a real, flesh-and-blood ghost! I got a fever of a hundred and four! My skin broke out in hives! Therefore, you, out of respect, should use a different word!"

"And how might I do that?"

"How the hell should I know? Use your own words when you speak, not mine."

"Look, I cannot and I will not use a different word. Because I thought of that word all by myself! And I can't think of another, at this precise moment!"

"Begging the pardon of all present," intervened the Marchese Manfredi Coniglio della Favara, with a mincing manner and raised-pinky regard for decorum, "but would the good cavaliere kindly explain what spectre he is talking about?"

~~~

Here a slight digression is in order. The proper place for the Marchese Coniglio della Favara, in terms of class and means, was, and had always been, among the members of the Circolo dei Nobili, or "Nobles' Circle," of Montelusa. However, on an unfortunate day the previous year, the statue of Saint Joseph happened to be passing under the great windows of the Circle, as it was the saint's feast day. The marchese went to one of the windows to watch the procession. As luck would have it, standing beside him was the Baron Leoluca Filò di Terassini, a rabid papist and tertiary of the Franciscan order. At that moment, for the first time in his life—having never before given the matter any thought—the marchese noticed how old Saint Joseph looked. After reflecting upon the age difference between Joseph and Mary, he came to a conclusion he had the poor judgment to express aloud:

"If you ask me, it was a marriage of convenience."

Now, by a twist of what we customarily call fate, the exact same thought had occurred to Baron Leoluca, plunging him promptly into a state of unfathomable anguish over the blasphemous idea that had just crossed his mind. Drenched in sweat, he grasped at once the point of the marchese's statement.

"Say that again, if you have the courage."

He issued his challenge with dark eyes smoldering like hot coals, twirling his right mustache with his index finger.

"Gladly."

"Wait. I should warn you: what you say may have consequences."

"I don't give a damn about any consequences. You see, to
me Saint Joseph looks decidedly too old to do it with Mary."

He was unable to elaborate any further, so swiftly had the
baron's slap arrived, every bit as swiftly as the kick that the
marchese quite unchivalrously dealt the baron's ballocks,
dropping him to the floor writhing and out of breath. The
two men then challenged each other to a duel, which they
fought with swords. The baron managed to inflict a superfi-
cial wound on the marchese, who meanwhile had resigned
from Nobles' Circle of Montelusa.

"You can't reason with those people," he said.

And so he had requested admission to the Vigàta Civic
Club and been enthusiastically welcomed, since, with all its
members being tradesmen, schoolteachers, clerks, or doctors,
no one had ever seen hide or hair of any aristocrats within
those walls. His presence added lustre to the place.

᭱᭱᭱

At the marchese's polite query, the cavaliere puffed his chest.

"I'm talking about Wogner! And his divine music! And
the spectre of his music, which scares all the other composers
to death! And upon which all of them, sooner or later, will
burn their fingers!"

"I've never heard of this Wogner," said Giosuè Zito, gen-
uinely astonished.

"Because you are an ignoramus! You've got less culture
than a mullet! I, for my part, have heard this music, which
the Signora Gudrun Hoffer played for me on the piano. And

it lifted me up to heaven! How the devil can anyone not know Wogner? Haven't you ever heard of his drama of the ghost ship, *The Flying Dutchman*?"

Giosuè Zito, having barely recovered from the previous slight, staggered, grabbing on to a small table to keep from falling.

"Ah, so you really do want to get on my nerves! Why the hell do you keep talking about ghosts?"

"Because that's what it's about, and it's a very great opera! What the hell do I care if it makes you shit your pants? The music is innovative, revolutionary! Like *Tristano*!"

"Ho ho ho!" said the Canon Bonmartino, a scholar of patristics, who was, as usual, cheating at a game of solitaire.

"And what do you mean by ho ho ho?"

"Oh, nothing," said the canon with a face so seraphic one could almost see two cherubs fluttering around his head. "It only means that *Tristano*, in Italian, means 'sad anus,' *ano triste*. And with a title like that, I can only imagine how beautiful the opera must be."

"Then you don't understand a blasted thing about Wogner."

"In any case the name is Wagner, W-A-G-N-E-R, and you pronounce the W like a V: *vahg-ner*. He's German, my friend, not English or 'Mercan. And, with all due respect to Signor Zito's mental health, he really is a ghost, this Wagner of yours. In fact, he died before he was even born. He's an abortion. His music is first-class shit, melodic diarrhea, all farts and caca. Stuff for the latrine. People who make serious music can't even manage to play it, believe me."

"Could I get a word in?" asked Antonio Cozzo, a secondary-school headmaster, from an armchair where he'd been reading the newspaper without a peep.

"By all means," said Bonmartino.

"Not to you," said Cozzo, "but to Cavaliere Mistretta."

"I'm all ears," said Mistretta, shooting him a fighting glance.

"I'd merely like to say something about *Il Trovatore*, the swan of Busseto's masterpiece. You know what I'm referring to?"

"Absolutely."

"So, Cavaliere, listen closely. First I'm going to take *Abietta zingara* and stick it in your right ear, then *Tacea la notte placida* and fit it snugly into your left, so you can no longer even hear your beloved Wogner, as you call him. Then I'm going to grab *Chi del gitano* and shove it deep into your left nostril, then *Stride la vampa* and put it into the right hole, so you can't even breathe. Finally, I'll make a fine bundle of *Il balen del tuo sorriso*, *Di quella pira*, and the *Miserere*, and shove the whole lot straight up your asshole, which, I am told, is fairly spacious."

Time, at the club, stood still. Then the chair next to the one in which Cavaliere Mistretta was sitting took flight and soared across the room towards the head of Headmaster Cozzo, who, expecting this sort of reaction, promptly stood up and sidestepped it as his right hand reached behind to the back pocket of his trousers where he kept his weapon, a Smith & Wesson five-shooter. But nobody present got alarmed. They all knew that Cozzo's gesture was a habit, a tic he repeated as many as three times a day in moments of heated discussion or rows. And it was likewise certain that never in a million years would Cozzo pull out his revolver to shoot at any living creature, human or animal.

"Come now, gentlemen!" said Commendator Restuccia,

a man of influence and few words, whom it was dangerous to contradict. "Shall we stop this foolishness?"

"It was he who provoked me!" said the cavaliere, trying to excuse himself as if he were still in grade school.

The commendatore, however, clearly annoyed, looked severely at the contending parties and said, in an unwavering voice:

"I said 'enough,' and that means 'enough.'"

The two men promptly pulled themselves together. Headmaster Cozzo picked up the chair that had grazed him, and Cavaliere Mistretta smoothed out his jacket.

"I want you to shake hands," the commendatore ordered them, and it would surely have been deadly not to obey. So they did, without looking each other in the eye, just as Tano, the waiter, was entering the room with a tray full of coffee, sesame seed biscuits, cannoli, lemon ices, jasmine sherbet, and almond-and-anise-flavored drinks. Tano began to distribute the refreshments according to the orders. Thus there was a moment of silence, and everyone present was able to hear Don Totò Prestia sing, just under his breath, *Una furtiva lacrima.*

In the silence, as they all ate and drank, they fell under the spell of Don Totò's voice, which had them blubbering like young calves with their throats slit. At the end, after the applause, Don Cosimo Montalbano, as if to return Totò the favor, replied in his own melodious voice by singing *Una voce poco fa.*

"Well, there certainly is some beautiful music around!" the Wogner supporter conceded to his adversaries, sighing.

"What are you trying to do, convert us?" Canon Bonmartino asked. "Just know that I won't give you my blessing. To me you will always remain a heretic, and you will go to hell when you die."

"Care to tell me just what sort of bloody priest you are?" Cavaliere Mistretta asked testily.

"Easy, gentlemen, easy," said the commendatore, and in the silence one didn't hear even the flies.

"On the other hand, Cavaliere, you're right," the canon continued. "There is plenty of beautiful music around. And yet we get the music of this Luigi Ricci, whom we know nothing about, shoved down our throats willy-nilly, simply because the authorities say so! It's sheer madness! We're supposed to let our ears suffer simply because the prefect orders it!"

The patristics scholar was so indignant that he threw down the cards of a game of solitaire that, by dint of cheating, he was actually about to win.

"You know what, gentlemen?" intervened Dr. Gammacurta, the physician. "Apparently this Ricci who wrote *The Brewer of Preston* has composed an opera that is a patent rehash of a work by Mozart."

At the sound of that name they all recoiled in horror. Merely mentioning the name of Mozart, inexplicably despised by Sicilians, was like uttering a curse or a blasphemy. In Vigàta, the only person to defend his music—which in everyone's opinion tasted neither of fish nor fowl—was Don Ciccio Adornato, the carpenter, but apparently he did so for personal reasons of his own which he was loath to discuss.

"Mozart?!" they all said at once.

But although they all spoke at the same time, they were not a chorus. Some said the name with disdain, some with pain, some in shock, some in astonishment, some in resignation.

"Yes, indeed, Mozart. I was told by someone who knows a thing or two. Apparently, about thirty-five years ago, at La Scala in Milan, this blockhead Luigi Ricci staged an opera called *The Marriage of Figaro*, which was an exact replica of a work by Mozart of the same title. And when it was over, the Milanese shat all over him. So this Ricci started crying and in tears went to seek consolation in the arms of Rossini, who, God knows why, was his friend. Rossini did what he was supposed to do and cheered him up, but he also let it be known to one and all that Ricci got what he had coming to him."

"And we're supposed to inaugurate our new Vigàta theatre with an opera by this mediocrity just because our distinguished prefect is besotted with him?" asked Headmaster Cozzo, menacingly touching the back pocket in which he kept his revolver.

"Oh Jesus, blessed Jesus," said the canon. "Mozart alone is a funeral, so we can well imagine what a bad copy of a bad original is like! What on earth was the prefect thinking?"

Since no one could answer this question, a thoughtful silence ensued. The first to break it was Giosuè Zito, who began to sing, very softly, so he wouldn't be heard in the street below:

"Ah, non credea mirarti . . ."

The Marchese Coniglio della Favara then followed:

"Qui la voce sua soave . . ."

And Commendator Restuccia, in a basso profondo, cut in:

"Vi ravviso, o luoghi ameni . . ."

At this point Canon Bonmartino got up from his chair,

ran over to the windows, and drew the curtains to make the room dark, while Headmaster Cozzo lit a lamp. The men then gathered in a semicircle around the light. And Dr. Gammacurta, in a baritone voice, intoned:

"*Suoni la tromba e intrepido . . .*"

The first to join him, as if written into the score, was the commendatore. One by one, all the others followed. Standing round, hands linked as in a chain, looking one another in the eye, they instinctively lowered the volume of their song.

They were conspirators. They had become so at that very moment, in the name of Vincenzo Bellini.

The Brewer of Preston, the opera by Luigi Ricci imposed on them by the prefect of Montelusa, would never play.

Would he try to raise the mosquito net?

Would he try to raise the mosquito net? the widow Concetta Lo Russo, née Riguccio, asked herself with trepidation, hidden behind the gauzy *tarlantana*, which in summer was spread around and over the bed to protect her from gnats, mosquitoes, *pappataci*, and horseflies.

At that moment the netting, with its light, veil-like mass, looked like a ghost hanging from a nail. The widow's generous bust was in the throes of a force-ten storm, with the portside tit drifting leeward to north-northwest, while the starboard one strayed in a south-southeasterly direction. The wife of a sailor who had drowned in the waters off Gibraltar, she was unable to think in any other terms than the nautical ones her husband had taught her after she married him at age fifteen only to don the widow's weeds at age twenty.

Good Lord, what pandemonium! What a night! What rough seas! Because of what had been arranged and was about to happen, her blood was already in motion, now receding and turning her pale, now rising up and spilling over the deck, turning her not so much red as purple. And, to top it all off, earlier that night she had listened in terror to loud cries coming from the new theatre that had been built opposite her building, then heard the blast of a trumpet, followed by a mad rush of people and horses, and a few gunshots to boot.

At that point she had become convinced that, with all the mayhem—whose cause escaped her—*he* would not dare come that night, and thus she could set her heart, and another part of her body, at rest. Resigned, she had undressed and gone to bed. Then, just as she was dozing off, she had heard a soft sound on the roof, then his slow, cautious steps over the tiles, followed by the muffled thud of his leap from the roof to her balcony, which she had left half open as agreed. Yet when she realized he had kept his word and in a few moments would enter her room, she felt overcome with shame. She couldn't remain lying on the bed half naked like some cheap whore, in her nightgown with nothing underneath. So she had bolted out of bed and hidden behind the great swath of *tarlantana*.

From there she heard him enter in darkness and close the French door to the balcony. She realized he was heading towards the bed and sensed his surprise at not finding her there, after feeling around with his hand several times. He began fidgeting beside the bedside table, and then she clearly heard him strike a match. She saw the wan light through the dense screen of the *tarlantana*, and finally the entire room was illuminated. He had lit the double candlestick. Only then, seeing him against the light, did the widow Lo Russo notice that he was completely naked—but when had he taken his clothes off? as soon as he'd entered? or had he walked over the tiled roof in that state?—and that between his legs hung some twelve inches of mooring rope, the kind used not for small boats but for steamships, a veritable hawser fastened to a curious sort of docking bollard with two heads. At that sight, a stronger wave swept over her and brought her to her knees. Despite the fog that had suddenly clouded her vision, she saw his silhouette turn sharply, sail straight to the spot where she was hiding, stop in front of the mosquito netting, crouch down to set the candlestick on the floor, seize the netting, and raise it abruptly. She, the widow, didn't know that his compass had not been his sight but his hearing, drawn by the plaintive, dovelike cooing she had begun to emit without even realizing it. He saw her kneeling before him, opening and closing her mouth like a mullet caught in a fishing net.

But her apparent shortness of breath did not prevent the widow from noticing that the mooring rope was changing form, slowly becoming a sort of rigid bowsprit. He bent down and, without a word, picked her up by her sweaty armpits, and hoisted her high over his head. She knew she was a rather heavy load for his shrouds, but he did not lose his balance and only lowered her slightly so that she could brace her legs around his back to anchor herself. Meanwhile the bowsprit had changed form again, becoming now a majestic mainmast, upon which the widow Lo Russo, firmly fastened thereto, began to quiver, flap, and pulsate like a sail full of wind.

⁂

Her husband had once told her a story he'd heard from a sailor who had gone a-whaling. In the cold waters of the North, the sailor said, there exists an extraordinary fish called a narwhal. Three times a man's size, it has a great ivory horn over three yards long between its eyes. Whosoever finds such an animal grows rich, because a pinch of the powder of that horn enables a man to do it fifteen times in a single night. At the time Signora Concetta hadn't believed the story. Now, however, she realized that it was all true, and that in her arms she was holding a little narwhal with scarcely twelve inches of horn, which was more than enough.

〰

The whole story had begun one Sunday, when she and her sister Agatina arrived late to Mass. The church was full, with not one of the wicker chairs the sacristan rented at half price untaken, and in front of them was a dense array of rough-looking men whom it would have been impolite to ask to step aside. The two women had no choice but to remain standing, far from the altar.

"We can just stand back here," Agatina had said to her.

Then the inner door to the church opened, and *he* entered. Concetta had never seen him before, but one look at him and she knew that for the next few minutes her ship would no longer answer the helm. He was beautiful, beautiful, an angel from heaven. Tall with thick blond curls and very lean, but only so lean as was proper in a healthy man, with an eye as blue as the sea and the other, his right eye, not there. That eye lay hidden under an eyelid that was sort of stuck to the part below, walled up. But this was not offputting; on the contrary, all the light of his extinguished eye poured into the other, making it gleam like a precious stone, a beacon in the night. She later learned from Agatina that he had lost the eye when he was stabbed with a knife during a scuffle. But this mattered little. She realized, at that exact moment, that all her navigational parameters had changed: he would, of necessity, become her port, even if she had to sail around Cape Horn. And he, too, had felt it, to the point that he turned his head to meet her eyes and dropped his anchor in their waters. They gazed at each other for a minute that lasted forever. Then, since by now the die was cast, he brought the fingers of his right hand together, *a cacocciola,* artichoke-like, and shook them up and down repeatedly.

It was a precise question:

What shall we do?

Concetta slowly stretched her arms away from her body, letting them hang down at her sides and turning the palms of her hands outwards, with a disconsolate look on her face.

I don't know.

It was a brief, rapid dialogue, expressed in minimal, barely sketched gestures.

∿

The violent jibbing maneuver he decided to make at one point took her by surprise. But she raised no objection and quickly obeyed. Having now become a boat, a lateen-rigged fisher, Concetta found herself with her prow on the pillow and her stern raised high to catch the wind blowing indeed astern, making her bounce from breaker to breaker and driving her irresistibly out to the open sea without compass or sextant.

∿

At Mass on the following Sunday she did everything human and divine in her power to arrive late, to the point that her sister Agatina had become impatient and called her a dawdler. Yet the moment she entered the church, the heavenly-blue beacon lit her, warmed her, and filled her with contentment. In its light and heat she felt rather like a lizard sunning itself on a rock.

Then he pointed his index finger at her.

You.

And then turned his index finger towards himself.

Me.

He clenched the same hand into a fist, brought the index finger and thumb together, then made a turning motion.

The key.

She shook her head from larboard to starboard and vice versa.

No, the key, no.

Indeed she could not give him the key to the house, because on the ground floor lived Mr. and Mrs. Pizzuto and upstairs, Signora Nunzia, who never slept. It was too risky. Someone might see him climbing the stairs.

He spread his arms, cocked his head to one side, smiled regretfully, then let his arms fall.

I guess that means you don't like me.

She felt as if she were sinking; her legs began to shake, her rosary fell to the floor. She bent down to pick it up and kissed it once, twice, letting her lips linger a long time on the crucifix and looking him straight in his one eye, which seemed to redden with fire, its blue turning to flame.

What are you saying? I'd like to have you on the cross so I could kiss you all over the way Mary Magdalen did to Christ.

〰〰

Now they were sailing close-hauled and smooth, the sea flowing softly as it rocked them like a cradle, with nary a wave to shake them up. They were a deckless coaster, he the sails and she the keel.

〰〰

At the third Mass he finally bent his index and middle fingers and touched his chest.

Me.

His fingers mimed a man walking.

I'll come to your place.

Her fingers formed the *cacocciola*.

How?

He raised his eye to the sky, kept it there a moment, then pointed his index finger upward.

From the roof.

Surprised and frightened, she made the *cacocciola* again.

How will you get up there?

He smiled, stiffened his left hand horizontally, and the index and middle fingers of his right hand mimed the motion of a man walking on it.

With a plank.

She looked dumbfounded and he smiled again. He was calm and resolute.

She formed a small circle with her forefinger and thumb, to indicate a clock, then gathered the fingers together again *a cacocciola*.

When?

He raised his open hands chest high, moving them lightly forward and back.

Wait.

~~~

"One of the parts that make up the hull," her dear departed had once explained to her, "is the bilge, a dark and smelly place where all the ship's filth ends up."

Then why, if it was a stinky, nasty place, was he trying to force his way in there?

~~~

Finally, on a recent Sunday, his index and middle fingers had mimicked a man walking.

I'm coming.

And without giving her time to respond, he held up three fingers.

In three days.

Again without pausing, he brought his two clenched fists together, then spread them outward and forward.

Open the French door to the balcony.

Once outside the church, she didn't have the courage to tell Agatina about all the conversations she'd been having each Sunday with the young stranger. She only asked:

"Do you know the young man we've been seeing in church, the one with only one blue eye?"

"Yes, he's one of the Inclima family. I think his name is Gaspàno. He's unmarried."

And they carried on talking about the young man until they got to Concetta's front door. As she was about to leave, Agatina said to her:

"Gaspàno is a wonderful boy. He'd be quite a catch for you."

～～～

Back at home, Concetta raced to the balcony of her bedroom to look outside and suddenly understood Gaspàno's audacious plan. Right behind her building, rising as high as the eaves, was a mountain of salt in the courtyard used as a depot by the Capuana firm. It would be relatively easy to lay a plank at the top of it, cross over to the tiled roof, and then ease oneself down into the double window.

She went back inside to make herself something to eat, but was unable. In the pit of her stomach was a sort of iron-hard stone. For the rest of the afternoon she dawdled about, not knowing what to do, fussing with things of no importance, such as sewing a button onto a shirt or adjusting the wick on a lamp. But everything she did she botched: her mind just wasn't in it.

She went to bed when it was still light outside, but couldn't fall asleep. All at once, when she least expected it, a waterspout began to form in a specific part of her body. At first there were little ripples on the water's surface brought on by a hot wind, hotter than the scirocco; then the gusts grew stronger and started spinning like a drill, with the point of the drill stuck to the same spot, turning and turning while the upper end of the waterspout broadened and invaded her body, which lay on the bed with arms and legs spread, making it shake all over.

Her dear departed had once told her that a waterspout can be made to deflate like a punctured football. One need only have the courage to approach the base of the twister with a caique, stick an oar through it, and mutter some mystical mumbo jumbo which, unfortunately, her dear departed had not revealed to her.

And so the caique that was her right hand bravely put out to sea and began to head south, pulled up alongside the cavity in the middle of her abdomen, skirted close round its edge, then proceeded to descend along a precise course, reached the center of the gulf created by her open legs, and cast anchor at the exact point where the waterspout rose up. As the caique rocked back and forth in those rough seas, she raised an oar—her index finger—and directed it carefully towards the tiny spot giving rise to all the agitation and, having found it, started striking it with the oar, harder and harder. Since she did not know the required mumbo jumbo, other perhaps more appropriate words came to her lips:

"Oh Gaspàno, oh Gaspàno, oh my dear Gaspàno . . ."

And all at once the waterspout collapsed and fell back into the gulf, turning into a dense, sticky froth.

᭡

He was no longer boat nor sea, but only a man, a bit tired, breathing heavily. Concetta licked his perfectly hairless chest, which looked like a little boy's. It tasted of salt, like that of her dear departed. He shut his eyes and squeezed her a little harder.

"Do you even know my name?" asked Concetta, whose eyelids were also getting heavy and starting to droop. It had been a long and tiring journey. Gaspàno did not answer her. He had already fallen asleep.

Get me Emanuele

"Get me Emanuele!" enjoined His Excellency the prefect of Montelusa, Cavalier *Dottor* Eugenio Bortuzzi, handing the bailiff a voluminous folder of documents he'd finished signing.

"He's already here; he's been waiting outside for the last half hour."

His Excellency frowned.

"You, Orlando, have always been a proper blockhead. You should have told me at once. Go."

No sooner had Orlando the bailiff walked out the door than Emanuele Ferraguto—better known in the province as Don Memè or, more simply, *u zu Memè* (that is, "Uncle Memè") especially by those not related, even remotely, to him—materialized in his place, blotting him out. It looked like a conjuring trick.

Fiftyish, tall, just the right amount of lean, and fairly well dressed, Don Memè, a broad, cordial smile on his face, made a slight bow, waiting for the prefect to signal to him to come forward.

~~~

Rumor had it that Don Memè had never stopped smiling in his life, not even when the police lieutenant lifted the sheet, five years back, to show him the tortured, mangled body of his son Gnazino, who hadn't made it to the age of twenty, stretched naked on a slab of marble. When, after the autopsy, Don Memè, still smiling, had politely asked the coroner to explain, the doctor informed him that, in his opinion, the young man's killers, before strangling him, had cut off his tongue, sawn off his ears, gouged out his eyes, and removed his dick and balls. In that order. And Don Memè had taken careful note of this order on a sheet of paper, using a copying pencil that he wet from time to time with the tip of his tongue. The message borne by that corpse in the very manner of its death was clear. Whoever killed the boy thought he talked too much and was a little too quick to bed the members of the fair sex, regardless of their tender age or marital status.

∿∿

In the two months that followed, Don Memè had devoted his energies to a complicated business transaction at the end of which, having ceded to others the rights to the Cantarella estate, he received in exchange, at his country house, his sons' two assassins, in such a condition that they could not lift so much as a finger.

Still according to rumor, Don Memè had wanted to see to the two men personally, having first donned some overalls so as not to stain his suit with blood. Taking out the sheet of paper on which he had written after speaking with the coroner, he hung it from a nail, and then proceeded to follow his notes blindly, showing not a whit of imagination. All the same, after cutting off their cocks and balls, he did have a burst of creative originality and strayed from the script. That is, he took the two dying men, laid them both across the back of a mule, and went and impaled them on the branches of a Saracen olive tree that stood on the now-ceded Cantarella estate.

When the corpses were discovered, by then eaten by dogs and crows, the police lieutenant, after a quick investigation, was convinced that two plus two equaled four and had Don Memè promptly arrested. That very same day, however, ten individuals, all above suspicion, from the town of Varo some thirty miles from Montelusa, had come running to testify that on the day of the double murder Don Memè was in their town celebrating the feast of San Calogero. Among those furnishing the alibi were the postmaster Ugo Bordin, from the Veneto; the *dottor* Carlo Alberto Pautasso, Esq., of Asti, director of the tax office; and the *ragioniere* Ilio Ginnanneschi, of Prato, an employee at the land registry.

"Ah, how splendid our unified Italy is!" Don Memè had exclaimed with a smile more cordial than usual, as the prison doors opened up to let him out.

~~~

Having completed his bow, Emanuele Ferraguto approached the broad prefectorial desk with some difficulty. In his right hand he was holding his English-wool cap and a packet, and in his left, a large parcel.

"Come in, come in, my good man," the prefect said jovially.

Having closed the door behind him with his shoe, Don Memè continued to walk with a slight limp in his right leg.

"Did you hurt yourself?" His Excellency inquired solicitously.

Don Memè managed to gesture "no" with his right forefinger without dropping his cap or the parcel.

"It's the roll," he whispered mysteriously, looking around

himself as he said it. He set the package on the desk. "These are cannoli from Sfiacca, the kind your wife likes so much."

Then it was the big, heavy parcel's turn.

"This, on the other hand, is a big surprise for you, Excellency."

The prefect looked at the parcel with eyes suddenly bright and hopeful.

"You don't say!" he said with a quaver in his voice.

"Oh, yes, indeed I do say!" Ferraguto said triumphantly.

"Is it *The Archaeological History of Sicily*, by the Duke of Serradifalco?"

"You're right on the money, sir. The books you've been looking for."

"And how did you ever find them?"

"I noticed that Scimè, the notary, owned a copy, so I politely asked him for them, and he gave them to me free of charge, as a gift to you." .

"Really? I must send him a note of thanks."

"Better not, Your Excellency."

"And why not?"

"That might be rubbing salt into the wound. It took some doing to persuade him, you know. The notary was rather fond of these books. I had to, well, to force him a little, to show him what was in his best interests."

"Ah," said His Excellency, running a loving hand over the parcel. "You know, Ferraguto, I'm going to tell you something. Books with dense writing bore me. They honfuse me. I understand images much better. And fortunately, Serradifalco's books are full of images."

Don Memè put an end to their cultural interlude.

"You must excuse me, Your Excellency, sir," he said as he started to unbutton his suspenders. In a single bound the prefect stood up, ran to the door, turned the lock twice, and put the key in his pocket. Ferraguto, meanwhile, extracted a long roll from his right trouser leg and set it down on the table, before buttoning himself back up in haste.

"That's what was making me walk all lopsided," he said. "I was worried the paper might wrinkle. It's a problem you don't have if you've got a *lupara* hidden in your trousers."

He laughed long and hard, alone, as His Excellency was opening the roll. It was the printer's proof of a placard announcing the forthcoming performance of the opera *The Brewer of Preston* to inaugurate Vigàta's new theatre. After reading it carefully and finding no mistakes, the prefect handed the roll back to Ferraguto, who slipped it back into his trouser leg.

"We're at the gates with stones in our hands, my friend."

"I don't understand, Your Excellency."

"It's a saying from my parts. It means there's not much time left. The opera will be staged the day after tomorrow—actually, in three days' time. And I'm very worried."

They allowed themselves a pause, looking one another in the eye.

"When I was a little kid," Emanuele Ferraguto said slowly, breaking the silence, "I liked to play with black *comerdioni*."

"Oh, really?" said the prefect, slightly disgusted, imagining some sort of black and hairy spider with which the child Ferraguto amused himself by pulling off its legs one by one.

"Yes," Ferraguto continued. "What do you call, in your parts, those toys that little kids make—"

"Ah, so it's a game?" the prefect interrupted him, visibly relieved.

"Yessir. You take a big sheet of colored paper, cut it into

the right shapes, glue two reeds to it with starch paste . . . then you attach it all to a string and send it up in the air."

"Ah! You mean a hite!" His Excellency exclaimed.

"Yes, exactly, sir, a kite. I used to fly them around Punta Raisi, near Palermo. Do you know the place?"

"What a silly huestion, Ferraguto! You know very well that I don't like to set foot out of the house. I know Sicily from picture hards. It's better than going there in person."

"Well, Punta Raisi's not a very good place for kites. Sometimes there was no wind and neither man nor God could make them rise. Other times there was wind all right, but as soon as the kite got up in the air it ran head-on into a current that would flip it over and send it crashing into the trees. I would dig in my heels and keep trying, but I was wrong. Do you get what I mean?"

"No, I don't."

Forever the Florentine dickhead, thought Ferraguto. He replied with a question.

"Would Your Excellency mind if I spoke Latin?"

The prefect felt a bead of sweat trickle down his back. From the very first time he had come up against *rosa-rosae* he had realized that Latin was his bête noire.

"Just between you and me, Ferraguto, I wasn't exactly the head of the class at school."

Don Memè beamed his legendary smile.

"What did you think I meant, Your Excellency? Here in Sicily, 'to speak Latin' means to speak clearly."

"And when you want to speak unclearly?"

"We speak Sicilian, Your Excellency."

"Go ahead, then, speak Latin."

"Your Excellency, why do you insist on trying to fly the

kite of *The Brewer of Preston* here in Vigàta, where the winds are unfavorable? Take it from a friend, which I'm honored to be—it won't fly."

At last the prefect grasped the metaphor.

"Whether it'll fly or not, people, in Vigàta, have to do what I tell them to do, what I order them to do. *The Brewer of Preston* will be staged, and it will have the success it deserves."

"Your Excellency, may I speak Spartan to you?"

"Oh my, what does that mean?"

"Speaking Spartan means using dirty words. Would you please explain to me why the hell you got it in your fucking head to force the Vigatese to watch an opera they don't want any part of? Does Your Excellency want to provoke another forty-eight, perhaps? A revolution?"

"Those are big words, Ferraguto!"

"No, sir, Your Excellency, those are not big words. I know these people. They are good, honest people, but if they're crossed they're liable to wage war."

"But, good God, why would the Vigatese wage war just to avoid listening to an opera?"

"It depends on the opera, Your Excellency."

"What are you trying to tell me, Ferraguto? That Vigàta has the best music critics in the world?"

"No, it's not that, sir. Except for two or three people, the Vigatese don't know a thing about music."

"So?"

"So the problem is that it was you, who are the prefect of Montelusa, who wanted this opera. And the Vigatese never like anything the Montelusans ever say or do."

"Is this some kind of joke?"

"No. They don't give a damn about the opera. But they

don't want it to be the person in charge of Montelusa and its province to lay down the law for Vigàta. You know what the canon Bonmartino—who's a priest everyone respects—said about this?

"No."

"He said that if the Vigatese accept the opera, next the prefect will feel entitled to tell them what they should eat and when they should shit."

"But that's absolute rubbish! It's a beautiful opera and they don't know what the hell they're talhing about!"

"Your Excellency, even if the opera had been written by God Almighty Himself with His band of angels—"

"Jesus Christ! We need to do more, Ferraguto! The opera must triumph! It has to behome an historic success! My hareer depends on it!"

"If you'd spoken to me sooner, Excellency, if you'd let me know your plans when there was still time, I could have taken action and given you my humble opinion on a few matters. Now I'm doing everything I possibly can."

"You must do more, Ferraguto. More. Even if it means . . ." He interrupted himself.

"Even if it means?" Ferraguto asked keenly.

The prefect sidestepped, realizing he was heading down a dangerous path.

"I'm counting entirely on you, on your sense of tact," he concluded, rising.

On the morning of the day

On the morning of the day he was killed, Dr. Gamma-curta was, as usual, at his medical office. He even spent the afternoon there, after a break for lunch and a brief half-hour nap. But he wasn't in his usual mood. Indeed, he was decidedly agitated, showing no patience with red-eyed children, losing his temper over tertian and quartan fevers alike, and flying off the handle when, for good measure, a man with a boil on the back of his neck was so afraid of the scalpel that he would not sit still for the doctor to lance it.

Then, when he was about to close the office and go home, somebody came running for him and told him that the sea had washed a half-drowned foreigner ashore. As soon as he saw the man, Gammacurta started cursing like a Turk.

"God bloody dammit! You call this half drowned?! Can't you see he's been dead for at least a week and that the fish have been eating him up? Call whoever the hell you want to call—the priest, the police, anybody—but leave me out of this!"

The reason for his bad mood—a strange thing in a man known far and wide as polite and well bred—lay in the fact that, come hell or high water, he had to go to the theatre that evening. At the club, he had made a solemn pledge, along with the other members, to make sure that the opera imposed on Vigàta by the prefect would end in boos and raspberries.

Being, moreover, little inclined by nature to appear in public, he had contemplated deserting the cause with the excuse that he needed to make a house call on someone gravely ill. But he had forgotten about his wife, with whom he had had a heated argument the previous day.

"But I had a dress made in Palermo for the occasion!" she had said.

The doctor had already seen the dress, and it looked to him like a carnival costume. Actually, even at Carnival, any self-respecting woman would have disdained to put it on. But it was clear that his missus had got it into her head to wear it.

"But the music is completely worthless."

"Oh, really? And how would you know? Have you suddenly become a music connoisseur? Anyway, I couldn't care less about the music."

"So why do you want to go?"

"Because Signora Cozzo is going."

The argument admitted no reply. Signora Cozzo, the headmaster's wife, was Signora Gammacurta's bête noire.

Naturally, nothing went right for him during the laborious process of getting dressed, owing in part to the deafening shouts in the next room, where his wife was getting made up with the help, apparently inept, of Rosina, the maid. The button to his collar refused to fit, falling on the floor three times; he could find only one of his gold cufflinks and spent an hour on the floor with his backside in the air before he managed to unearth the other under the chest of drawers; and his patent leather shoes were too tight.

᷍᷍᷍

Now he was finally at the theatre, in the third row of the orchestra, beside his wife, who looked like a cassata—a rustic ice cream speckled with colorful candied fruit—and was smiling beatifically because the dress of Signora Cozzo, sitting two rows behind them with her husband, was not as striking as her own. The doctor looked around. His associates from the club, with whom he exchanged greetings, smiles, and nods of understanding, had all positioned themselves strategically between the boxes and the pit.

∿

The stage décor represented the courtyard of a brewery in the town of Preston, England, according to a small flyer that had been distributed to everyone upon entering the theatre. On the left-hand side was the façade of a two-story house with a staircase on the outside; on the right was a great cast-iron gate; and in the background, a brick wall with a door in the middle. There were wheelbarrows, sacks full of who-knows-what, and shovels and baskets scattered about helter-skelter.

The music struck up, and a man in a gray apron appeared—Bob the foreman, according to the flyer. Looking all cheerful, he started ringing a bell. At once six people wearing the same aprons entered from behind the gate, but instead of getting down to work, they lined up at the edge of the stage in front of the audience. From their faces and gestures they looked even happier than their foreman, who turned to them, opened his arms, and intoned:

> *"Friends! To the brewery*
> *we merrily run!"*

The workers looked like they were in seventh heaven.

> *"We merrily run!"*

they all sang together, raising their hands.

> *"With barley and hops*
> *we make our beer!"*

The six people in aprons then started jumping for joy.

> *"We make our beer!"*

Bob the foreman then ran in a great circle around the courtyard, showing off the equipment.

> *"Of all the trades*
> *ours has no peer."*

The six people embraced and patted one another noisily on the back.

> *"Ours has no peer."*

Then Bob, running from a wheelbarrow to a sack and from the sack to a pile of baskets, sang:

> *"We make a drink*
> *that brings good cheer."*

"Yeah, cheer for *you!*" a voice yelled from the seats just under the ceiling. "To me it tastes like piss! I'll take wine anyday!"

The voice drowned out even the music. But the chorus didn't let it bother them and continued singing.

"That brings good cheer."

At this point somebody got angry in earnest. It was Don Gregorio Smecca, a trader in whole and slivered almonds, but above all a pig-headed man.

"Why are these six assholes always repeating the last lines? What do they think, that we're a bunch of savages? We can understand whatever there is to understand at the first go, without any repetition!"

Lollò Sciacchitano, who was sitting in the gallery but far from his friend Sciaverio, the one who had declared his dislike of beer, seized the moment.

"Hey, Sciavè, why are they all so cheerful?" he asked in a voice that would have been audible at sea during a squall.

"Because they're going to work," was Sciaverio's reply.

"What bullshit!"

"Go ahead, ask them yourself."

Sciacchitano stood up and addressed himself to the seven people on stage.

"I beg your pardon, gentlemen, but would you please give me a straight answer? Why are you so happy to be going to work?"

This time there was a certain confusion on stage. Two of the chorus shaded their eyes with their hands to shield them from the stage lights and looked towards the gallery, but the conductor's baton immediately called them back to order.

In the royal box, Bortuzzi, the prefect, noticing that things were taking a bad turn, felt his blood rising. Gesturing angrily to Police Lieutenant Puglisi behind him, he said:

"Arrest those hooligans! At once!"

Puglisi didn't feel like obeying the order. He knew that the slightest incident might trigger an uprising.

"Look, Your Excellency, I'm sorry, but there's absolutely no ill will or intention in what they're doing. They're not troublemakers. I know every last one of them. They're good, law-abiding people, believe me. It's just that they've never been in a theatre before and don't know how to behave."

It worked. The prefect, who was drenched in sweat, did not insist.

Meanwhile, from the left-hand staircase appeared Daniel Robinson, the owner of the brewery. He was even jollier than the others and in the end declared that day a holiday, because he was about to marry a girl named Effy. This news made the others practically faint with joy. Bob intoned:

> "What better choice to make than she?
> Who more virtuous and pretty?"

The six clad in aprons once again did not fail to repeat:

> "Who more virtuous and pretty?"

Don Gregorio Smecca could no longer contain himself. "Bah! What a bore! I'm leaving, good night!"
He stood up and left, leaving his wife in the lurch.

Meanwhile the people on stage were describing Effy as a "most precious gem" and as the "emblem of love." And so Daniel Robinson started handing out money to everyone, ordering them to have a big celebration.

> "Look for instruments, look all around,
> let flutes, timbals, and horns resound."

"No need to look anywhere for horns. They grow all by themselves," said a voice again from the gallery. A few people laughed.

"But isn't a timbal that thing you make for me with rice, meat, and peas?" Dr. Gammacurta asked his wife in all seriousness.

"Yes."

"So what the hell has it got to do with flutes and horns?"

At last the theatre fell briefly silent. The workers had all gone off in search of instruments and people to invite to the celebration. Daniel Robinson, though there was nobody beside him, started gesturing mysteriously towards Bob as if wanting to tell him a secret. Bob drew near, and the boss revealed to him that before the day was over, his own twin brother, George, who hadn't been seen in those parts for two years, would arrive. George was a military man and not a very peaceable sort. Bob looked doubtful.

"And he's coming here?"

Daniel turned pensive then replied:

"I hope so, with his unpleasant vocation
of living by the balls . . ."

Hearing of the twin brother George's rather peculiar job, the male contingent of the audience held its collective breath. Some thought they hadn't understood correctly and sought clarification from the person beside them. Daniel, as the music required, repeated the declaration of his brother's occupation in a higher register:

"With his unpleasant vocation
of living by the balls . . ."

This time the laughter burst out immediately, spanning
the entire hall from rows A to U and featuring throat-rasping
chortles, sneezing guffaws, gurgling giggles, smothered hic-
cups, starting motors, piglike squeals, and other similar man-
ners of laughing. And, as a result, the sung explanation of
George's odd vocation was completely lost.

". . . of living by the balls of the cannon."

The laugh that Cavaliere Mistretta tried to suppress turned
out to be the most clamorous of all. As the cavaliere was asth-
matic, he found himself gasping for air, and in his attempt to
recover his breath, he inhaled so deeply that it came out sounding exactly like a foghorn. And yet in spite of the blast, he did
not recover his breath but began to flail about, wildly grasping
and slapping at the people around him. His wife got scared and
started shouting, others came running, and one of them, a little
more alert than the rest, hoisted the cavaliere onto his shoulders
and carried him into the lobby with Signora Mistretta trailing
behind him and wailing like one of the three Marys.

At first Dr. Gammacurta congratulated the cavaliere in
his mind, thinking that the whole thing was an act Mistretta
was putting on to disrupt the musical performance, in accordance with their agreement. But then he realized he was act-
ing in earnest.

◆◆◆

On the stage, meanwhile, Effy, the fetching bride-to-be, popped
out, a great big woman at six foot six with hands that looked like

shovels and a nose you could grab on to in high winds. Under this nose was the dark shadow of a mustache that a generous application of makeup was unable to hide. She moved about, moreover, in long strides, heels clattering noisily behind her.

Giosuè Zito's wife, Signora Filippa, sat in serene bliss. Having been born deaf, she heard none of what was being said either in the pit or onstage. For her, everything was unfolding in angelic harmony. At the sight of the giant soprano, however, her curiosity was aroused.

"Giosuè, who's that?"

Upon Effy's entry onto the stage, Giosuè Zito, for his part, had felt alarmed.

They're not playing straight, he thought. *There's something fishy going on here. That's not a woman. That's a man.*

"That's George, the twin brother!" he replied with conviction, and, naturally, he had to shout it for his wife to hear him.

Laughter broke out again, even though Giosuè Zito's contribution to the opera's downfall had been completely unintended.

Apparently panic-stricken by everything that was happening in the audience and by what she had managed to hear while getting ready to enter the stage, the soprano playing the part of Effy displayed, in her face, eyes, and convulsive hand-wringing, and in the jerky movements of her considerable bulk, the exact opposite of what she was supposed to express: joy over her imminent marriage. At the maestro's imperious gesture, she began singing in a voice that was like an oil lamp with no wick:

"I too know a bit of the art
of sweet words and coy smiles,
and can win a man's heart

with glances and other wiles:
thousands of lovers and suitors
I've seen swoon over me . . ."

At this point the voice of Lollò Sciacchitano was again heard from the gallery.

"Hey, Sciavè, would you ever swoon over a cow like that?"

Sciaverio's reply boomed stentorian:

"Not even after thirty years of hard labor, Lollò!"

Dr. Gammacurta felt sorry for the woman onstage, who bravely kept on singing. He felt that it wasn't right. The poor woman was trying to earn her living and had nothing to do with the Vigatese, the Montelusans, and that shit of a prefect.

"I'm going to go see how Cavaliere Mistretta is doing," he said to his wife. And he got up from his seat, made the four people blocking his path to the aisle stand up, then headed towards the lobby.

Ladies and, so to speak, gentlemen

"Ladies and, so to speak, gentlemen. It was suggested to my wife, Concetta, that I should give a lecture on Luigi Ricci, the composer of the opera *The Brewer of Preston*, which will be performed several days hence in Vigàta's new theatre, the pride and glory of that delightful town. And I have to give this lecture, like it or not, because I can never deny my wife anything. Anything at all, believe me. Why, you may ask?"

He heaved a sort of sob, extracted a red-checked handkerchief, bobbed his head back and forth several times as if to ask for the compassion of those present, blew his nose with a powerful blast, put the handkerchief back into the pocket of his coat and tails, and, with a bitter smile on his face, resumed speaking.

"My mother used to ask me, over and over: 'Could you please explain to me how you got it into your head to marry that girl? Concetta is thirty years younger than you. Ten years after your marriage, you'll already be sixty, while she'll still be only thirty. To keep her from running away and to keep the family in peace, you'll have to become worse than a servant, ready to bend over backwards for her every slightest whim.' How right the good woman was, God rest her soul!

Her words were the Gospel truth. To give you an example: I knew nothing about this Luigi Ricci, and I truly didn't give a damn about him or his music, if you'll excuse my saying so. At any rate, there aren't many things that appeal to me anymore. But it was hopeless. You *have* to give this lecture, the wife commanded, or else . . . And don't I know what 'or else' means! But, enough, let's forget about that. And where did my wife get this idea? You all know that Concetta is a close friend of the wife of His Excellency, the prefect Bortuzzi. Do you see the problem now? Is it clear? This is why I am now standing in front of you like a jackass."

Sitting in the front row beside the prefect's gilded chair, which was luckily absent the latter's august form owing to some unexpected and unavoidable tasks of governance, Don Memè Ferraguto had been feeling lost for the past several minutes, ever since, in fact, the speaker had begun talking. Indeed he felt more lost than he ever had in his life, though he had never lacked occasions for feeling that way. For it was he who had had the brilliant idea to tell the prefect that his own wife, Luigia, known to intimates as Giagia, should speak to Signora Concetta, wife of *dottor* Carnazza, headmaster of the grammar school of Fela. Friends he had asked for advice on the matter had recommended Carnazza as the most refined of musical connoisseurs, without, however, mentioning—the bastards—that the headmaster was also, indeed perhaps to a greater degree, the most refined of wine connoisseurs. And to think that His Excellency himself had warned him of this.

"Are you sure we han hount on this Harnazza?"

"Of course, Your Excellency. Why do you ask?"

"Because my spouse told me that Signora Harnazza honfided to her that the headmaster goes at it rather often."

"Goes at what, Your Excellency?"

"What the hell do you think he goes at, Ferraguto? He goes at the bottle, and when he does, he talks rubbish."

"Don't you worry, Excellency. I'll keep after him like his own shadow. I won't even let him drink water."

And there he was now, in front of everyone, drunk as a skunk. Never mind talking too much—he was speaking in tongues like the Sybil of Cumae. No doubt he had knocked back one of the bottles he kept hidden in the large pockets of the overcoat he put on before leaving home, and had done it when he'd asked for permission to go to the restroom a few minutes before beginning his lecture. Chock-full of wine as he always had to be, a mere whiff of the cork had been enough to set him off.

~~~

"And then and then and then . . . this Luigi Ricci was born one fine day in Naples, one *hot* day, actually, since he was born in the month of July, in 1805. And as if the misfortunes the Neapolitans are customarily subjected to weren't enough, four years later his brother Federico was also born, soon to become a composer as well.

"But there's something important that needs to be said, so please pay attention—Jesus Christ! Why are you laughing? If you carry on I'll throw you straight out of the classroom, understand? So. The father of the two boys was one Pietro Ricci, who was not, however, Neapolitan but Florentine by birth, if you know what I mean—just like a certain person we all know—and he played the piano the way everyone plays piano these days, like my wife, for instance. A dime a dozen, know what I mean? But since my dear wife is pretty, everyone always tells her she plays like an angel, whereas, as far as I know, angels play winds and brass, never the piano. Speaking of which, is there anyone present who could sell me a used but good piano? The one my wife made me buy got smashed up when we moved house from Bìcari, where I taught Latin, to Fela. Not a particularly fancy piano, mind you, just so long as it plays, or can play what she's going to play on it . . . Now, where was I? Where the hell was I? Ah, yes, I was talking about Luigi Ricci. Well, he studied music and started composing. The first crap he wrote—oh, I'm sorry, that just slipped out—anyway, his first compositions, for whatever reason, were very successful. Theatres all over Italy wanted him, from Rome to Naples to Parma to Turin to Milan. And, since he couldn't manage to keep up with all the music they were asking him to write, he started copying stuff wherever he could find it, the way some of my pupils do. There's one, in fact, who seems to take his lessons from the devil himself. You know what he does, when I give them Latin dictation? He goes . . . Where does he go? But what's this got to do with anything? Ah, yes, Luigi Ricci. Anyway, the applause kept coming for Ricci, and he wasted no time; he wrote and copied and slept with all the sopranos who came within his grasp. In Trieste he made the acquaintance of three Bohemian women—no, actually, that makes them sound like they were made of glass, or crystal; in fact it would be better to say *from* Bohemia—so, these three women from Bohemia were sisters, their family name was Stolz, and individually they were Ludmilla, Francesca, and Teresa. The last one, Teresa, was the same angelic soprano—in this case *truly* angelic—known for interpreting the operas of Verdi, the swan of Busseto. And apparently this Teresa would fairly often turn into Leda for the swan. Ha ha ha! Get it? Why aren't you laughing? Don't you know the story of Leda and the swan? No? Well, I'm not going to tell it to you, if you're that ignorant. Anyway, to go on—actually, to go backwards— Luigi Ricci started dipping his biscuit with Ludmilla and Francesca. And apparently he was dipping with Teresa, too, but only when the other two cups weren't within reach. Heh, heh. Between Ludmilla and Francesca, little Luigi didn't know which one to choose. He would lie awake at night, between the two women, eaten alive by doubt, and so, in order not to offend either of them, he would be fair and lend his services to both. In the end he married Ludmilla and had a son with Francesca. These sorts of things happen. You don't believe it? I swear to you that the exact same thing happened once, the exact same way, to a friend of mine, whom I see seated here, in the audience, next to his worthy wife. He had two women, he told me once in confidence; and with the one, he talked, and with the other, he did you-know-what. Then he had a daughter with the one he talked to. So, my question is: With what did my friend do his talking?"

◂◂◂

Patanè the broker, sitting in the fourth row, recognized himself at once in the words of Headmaster Carnazza and had such a fright that he felt like he had been punched in the stomach. He doubled over.

"What's wrong? Do you feel sick?" asked his wife, worried.

"It's nothing, nothing. A little acid, that's all. The suckling goat didn't agree with me," the broker replied, wishing that an earthquake, waterspout, or some other sort of natural disaster would stop Carnazza from continuing his talk. But the wine in the headmaster's veins and head kept following an unpredictable course. In the end, Carnazza did not name his friend.

~~~

"Begging your pardon, I shall pick up Ariadne's thread again—or, actually, the thread of the subject, if you will, which is the same thing. Yes indeed. Ariadne's thread, which leads one back to the subject, is made up of conjunctions. Have you ever noticed? If you can grab a hold of one and then follow the others that come after, you'll find your way out of the labyrinth. So, Ricci. Luigi Ricci, after all this, died a few years ago, and in Prague, no less. He made trouble everywhere he went. With a little help from his brother, perhaps. Which brings us to *The Brewer of Preston*. It was first performed in Florence, in 1847. So here we are again. In Florence. Get my point? You can see how it all makes sense. Luigi's father is Florentine, the first performance is Florentine, and you-know-who—who happens to govern us—is Florentine. I believe that the man who wrote the libretto, a certain Francesco Guidi, copied it from a French author, one Adolf Adam, who in 1838 had staged a comic opera at— where else?—the Opéra Comique . . . Wait a minute, I've lost my train of thought. So, Guidi copies an opera by Adam in French but with the same title. Enough said. And at this point it seems to me we're talking about copying like there's no tomorrow, copying lyrics, copying music . . . I'd like to develop a concept here. I need to go to the bathroom; my belly feels like it's been turned upside down."

~~~

He went out staggering as if he was on rough seas, rolling one minute, pitching the next. Don Memè then made a desperate decision: *I'm going to go after him*, he thought, *follow him into the lavatory, and the moment he sits down on the pot, I'll bash him in the head with the butt of my pistol and leave him there for dead.* As he was getting up to do this, he suddenly found the Marchese Coniglio della Favara planted in front of him.

"Thanks, Don Memè," the marchese said with a grin. "I didn't know you were on our side, in spite of everything."

The old scarecrow's right, Don Memè suddenly thought with a shudder.

Seeing how things were going, the prefect might think it was he, Memè, who had pulled the wool over his eyes, proposing a lecture that was starting to look like a dirty trick, since it was entirely in agreement with those opposed to *The Brewer of Preston*.

After eyeing Don Memè a good while, always maintaining his grin, the marchese withdrew to go and talk to other guests. The lecture, in fact, was being held in the music room of his own palazzo in Montelusa, just as Ferraguto had explicitly asked him. And the marchese had not let him down. The only time he did deny a favor to Don Memè, some two hundred Saracen olive trees on his property had, by curious coincidence, gone up in flames.

Don Memè looked around. Not a single Montelusan aristocrat had shown up. The cornuti. And perhaps, given Carnazza's drunkenness, it was better that way. There was a surplus of bourgeois, of course, and many public employees, but most were already leaving, especially the churchgoing ladies, scandalized by the headmaster's language and dragging their husbands behind them. Who, it must be said, acquiesced rather reluctantly, as they would rather have stayed to see how the farce would end. Some thirty people remained.

Not knowing what to decide, whether to go and kill

Carnazza or let himself sink blissfully into the shit pile he had helped to create, Don Memè started staring at the frescoes on the ceiling. At a certain point he gave a start and shook himself from his torpor, worried. How long had it been since Carnazza left the room, anyway? He hadn't had time to answer his own question when the marchese reappeared before him.

"I beg your pardon, *carissimo* Ferraguto, but don't you think Professor Carnazza is taking advantage of my guests' patience and mine?"

Fucking marchese, thought Don Memè. *He wants to savor my ruin to the very end!*

⋙

There was no sign of Carnazza in the little toilet chamber. Indeed, a servant who was planted in front of the bathroom door declared that Headmaster Carnazza had not availed himself of its services. Don Memè asked another servant standing at the end of a long corridor if he had seen Carnazza pass that way, but the domestic said no. He opened a door or two and found nothing. Cursing, he returned to the music room and approached the marchese, who was now laughing in his face disrespectfully and with no restraint.

"I can't find him," said Don Memè.

The marchese promptly assembled all servants, family members, and guests who wished to take part in a sort of game. For the headmaster must certainly have got lost somewhere inside the palazzo, since the doorman swore by all that was holy that he had seen no one leave the building. They searched for hours and hours, equipped with lamps, candles, and lanterns. They descended into the cellars, went up into the attics, and spent the entire night searching, in part because around midnight, the marchese had the good idea to call for a recess and send for a round of spaghetti with pork followed by four roast suckling goats. They fell to with gusto, but never did manage to unearth Carnazza. He had vanished the instant he walked out the door of the music room.

"When he gets over his bender, he'll resurface," the marchese said at the first light of dawn.

⌁

He turned out to be a bad prophet. Headmaster Antonio Carnazza never resurfaced. Someone ran into him, or thought he saw him, years later in a seedy tavern in Palermo, reciting verse by Horace to a crowd even more wine-soaked than he. The Baroness Jacopa della Mànnara swore she had seen him among the ruins of the Greek theatre at Taormina, wearing a crown of vine leaves on his head and noisily declaiming verses of Catullus. The only sure thing was that a few years later, his wife had a declaration of presumed death drawn up and was thus accorded the status of widow. After duly waiting out the period of mourning, she remarried a nephew of Prefect Bortuzzi who happened to be in Sicily for a hare-hunting party.

⌁

(A slight digression is in order here, not because the narrator so wishes, but because the story itself imperiously demands it. In 1942, during the war, Montelusa, unlike Vigàta, which was repeatedly bombed by the Americans, suffered only one bombing, but it was a devastating one. In the course of this act of war, Palazzo Coniglio was half destroyed. Once the all-clear sounded, the rescue squads—not to mention a handful of people with serious intentions of getting their hands on some of the treasures that according to local lore were in that palazzo—scattered in every direction to look for possible dead and wounded. In the attic of the west wing, which was miraculously left standing, a skeleton of a man in formal dress was found inside a trunk, surely dead of natural causes, since there was no visible trace of violence.

It was a special sort of trunk that opened on the outside but which, once closed, released a spring that made it impossible to reopen from the inside. Anyone who might climb into it, even as a joke, could never come back out again without outside help. Beside the remains were found some sheets of paper with some barely visible, incomprehensible writing on them. With great effort one could make out a name that looked like Luigi Picci or Ricci.)

Turiddru Macca, son

Turiddru Macca, son of Gnà Nunzia and a stevedore who worked at the port, had gone to bed at nightfall, after the Angelus bell, as he had done for years, aching all over from the toil of loading more than two hundred full sacks a day onto his shoulders and carrying them from wharf to boat. He had slept barely six hours when he was awakened by a loud knocking on the door of the hovel where he lived with his entire family, a single room some twelve by twelve feet on the ground floor with one small window, beside the door, as the sole source of air.

"Turiddru Macca!"

He sat up in bed, scared, and set his hand down on the mattress, but only ended up crushing the face of his son Pasqualino, who moaned in his sleep. The knocking grew louder.

"Turiddru Macca!"

Turiddru stretched his legs in order to get up and in so doing kicked his daughter Annetta, who fell out of bed but, being accustomed to falling, climbed back in without even opening her eyes. The knocking continued, leaving Turiddru no time to collect himself. He slid out of bed, stepping directly on the liver of his son Minicuzzo, who was sleeping on the floor. Staggering blindly towards the window, he stumbled and very nearly fell on his son Antonino, who was asleep on a straw pallet.

"Turiddru Macca!"

His wife, Carolina, opened one eye and sat up, careful not to suffocate her six-month-old daughter Biniditta, who had fallen asleep still attached to one of her tits.

"Whoozat? *Madonna santa*, who could it be at this hour?"

"I dunno. Shut up and sleep," Turiddru ordered her, feeling nervous.

When he opened the window, a blast of frigid air assailed him. The night had taken a turn for the worse.

"Whoozat?"

"Iss me, Turi, Gegè Bufalino."

"What the hell do you want at this hour? What's going on?"

"Wha'ss going on is your mother's house is on fire. Hurry up and get dressed."

Gegè Bufalino was someone who was never to be trusted, whether his belly was full of wine or he hadn't drunk a drop.

"Gegè, I'm warning you: if it turns out you're making this thing up, I'm gonna bust your ass."

"I swear it on my own eyeballs! Lemme die by murder if I's lyin'," Gegè vowed. "Iss the holy Gospel truth."

Turiddru got dressed in a hurry. The night was pitch-black, but every now and then a flash dispersed the darkness. Towards the center of town, around the new theatre, and right behind it, where his mother Gnà Nunzia's house was, a great big red glow lit up the sky. Fire, no doubt about it. Turiddru started running.

✦✦✦

Once past the cordon of mounted soldiers arrayed in a circle around the area on fire, Herr Hoffer decided, at a glance, that there was nothing more to be done for the new theatre. Fire had already eaten up half of it. He ran behind the building: a small alley not three yards wide was all that separated the theatre from a two-story house that itself was ablaze.

"*Uber hier!* Dis way!" Hoffer cried to his men, who arrived in a flash with the fire-extinguishing machine.

A man approached holding a wet handkerchief over his nose to protect himself from the smoke.

"I'm Lieutenant Puglisi, police. Who are you, and what are you trying to do?"

"Mein name ist Hoffer, I been ein engineer. Minink engineer. I haff a machine I infented to outputten fires hier. Will you helf me?"

"Yes, of course," said the lieutenant, who'd given up hope when he'd seen the damage. He was quick to accept anything, even chickenshit, that might be of use.

"Goot. You must ko und make a chain of men vit buckets von hier to the sea. They take the sea vater and put it in the machine. The machine alvays neets new vater."

"All right," said Puglisi, who ran off to organize the effort.

As his men stoked the wood fire under the boiler to create the pressure necessary to force the cold water out, Hoffer noticed that behind him stood a group of motionless, almost statue-like people, consisting of a man of about fifty, a woman of about forty, a youngster of about twenty, and a girl of about sixteen. The two males were wearing woolen undershirts and undershorts. Apparently they had given their clothes to the women, who, being dressed only in nightgowns, were in fact covering their pudenda with men's trousers and jackets.

"You liff in dis haus?" the engineer asked the motionless group.

The group came to life.

"We're the Pizzuto family," the four said in unison.

The fifty-year-old man took half a step forward and spoke.

"I'm Antonio Pizzuto," he said in a drawling, whiny voice. "We live on the ground floor of this house. When it caught fire we were sleeping with the windows closed."

"With the windows closed," echoed the others.

"Because earlier the place had turned into a shithouse," Antonio Pizzuto continued.

"A shithouse," repeated the others.

Engineer Hoffer was dumbfounded, being rather unfamiliar with classical studies. He didn't realize that the Pizzuto family was essentially composed of a coryphaeus and an accompanying chorus.

"Exkuse me?" he said.

"Yessirree, a shithouse. With all this bullshit about inaugurating the theatre, carriages started arriving, dozens of them, from Montelusa, from Montechiuso, from Cavàra, from Fela, and wherever the hell else they came from."

"Wherever the hell else they came from," the chorus chimed.

"Fact is, the servants and coachmen, whenever nature called, would come behind the theatre to shit and piss in the little alleyway. And it got to stinking so bad that we had to close the windows."

"We had to close the windows."

"And that's why we didn't realize in time what was happening. It's a good thing my son, Nenè, got thirsty and went to drink a glass of water. Otherwise we would have been burnt to death, all of us."

"Burnt to death, all of us! Oh! Oh!" moaned the chorus.

Meanwhile the first buckets of seawater were arriving, as the chain of men had been quickly assembled by Lieutenant Puglisi. Now the work could begin. Hoffer's men took up their positions as if they had trained long and hard. Gripping the pump hose firmly, two of them directed it towards the entrance of the house in flames.

"*Achtung!*" the engineer shouted. "Prepare to extinkuish!"

Looking at his men, he felt a lump of emotion rise up in his throat.

"Open!"

Nardo Sciascia, hearing the order, opened the cold-water valve. At once a violent jet emerged. The two men holding the hose staggered, then directed the stream towards the blaze. In his excitement the engineer started dancing, first on one foot, then the other, like a bear.

~~~

By dint of curses, obscenities, and shouts, Turiddru Macca managed to get past the cordon of soldiers on horseback. At once he found himself in front of his mother's burning house, eyes full of tears from sorrow as much as from the gusts of acrid smoke. The fire was still for the most part confined to the ground floor, but evil tongues were rising towards the great window on the story above, where his mother had stood many times and waved at him. Turiddru was crying for fear of the danger his mother was in, but also for the beautiful apartment that was going up in smoke, those three rooms and kitchen where he and his family had hoped to move, out of their hovel and into more comfort and space, after Gnà Nunzia died—at the proper time, of course, in accordance with the will of God.

"Where's my mother?" he frantically asked Puglisi. "Where's Gnà Nunzia?"

"We haven't seen her yet," said Puglisi.

"But is she alive?"

"How should I know? We would have to enter the building, but as you can see, we can't even get close."

~~~

"Stop! Halt!" the engineer suddenly shouted at his men, and Nardo closed the valve. Hoffer had noticed that the buckets of water weren't arriving fast enough. The amount of water shooting out the hose was far greater than that which was being put in, and thus the pressure gauge was rising perilously. The boiler was in danger of exploding.

"*Schnell!* Qvick! You must verk fester! Vater, vater! More vater!" the engineer kept shouting at the long human chain, and at last the buckets began to move more rapidly.

At that moment the great window of the apartment inhabited by Gnà Nunzia suddenly opened and an elderly woman in a white nightgown appeared. The pale apparition raised her arms to the heavens.

"*Gesuzzu beddru! Madunnuzza santa!* He said there would be fire, and fire it is!"

"Mamà! Mamà!" Turiddru called to her.

The old woman made no sign of having heard him. She vanished into the house.

"*Schnell!* Qvick!" an excited Hoffer cried loudly. "Ve must safe dis olt voman!"

He noticed that the water-level gauge was now where it was supposed to be. Perhaps it would have been best to wait just a little longer, but there was no time to lose. The joy he felt at that moment at being able to save a human life with his invention made him commit a fatal mistake. Indeed, for a brief moment Hoffer forgot he was in Vigàta, Sicily, and lost control of the mechanism in his brain that was constantly translating his thoughts from German into Italian.

"*Schnell! Kaltes Wasser!*" he cried.

Nardo Sciascia, who was about to reopen the cold-water valve, stopped in midmotion and gave him a puzzled look.

"*Kaltes Wasser! Kalt! Kalt!*" roared the engineer.

Now, since the Italian word for "hot" is *caldo*, an inevitable misunderstanding occured.

"He wants the hot water! Pressure!" Sciascia cried to Cecè Consolo, who was at the back of the machine. Cecè turned the pressure knob and jumped backwards. At once a violent jet of steam and boiling water gushed from the back of the boiler. The nearly statue-like group of the Pizzutos, who were still standing behind the machine, was blotted out by a white cloud from which some very loud Greek-chorus-like laments resounded.

"Mistake! Mistake! I vant colt vater! Colt!" Hoffer screamed.

When the white cloud dissipated, the Pizzutos were on the ground moaning and rolling around with burns of varying degrees. Puglisi came running with two of his men.

"Quick!" the policeman said to the men. "Go get some help, put them in a carriage, and take them to Dr. Gamma-curta's."

"Dr. Gammacurta is nowhere to be found," said one of them.

"Then take them to Dr. Addamo."

"Addamo is up to his neck with all the ladies in hysterics

over the pandemonium that broke out at the theatre, not to mention all the people who got hurt when Don Memè started shooting."

"Don't give me any crap! I don't want to hear about it! Just take these people to Addamo. He'll understand right away that they're seriously injured."

Meanwhile Gnà Nunzia had reappeared at the great window. In her hand she held a sheet of paper that she began to shred into many little pieces, which she then tossed as far as she could with the help of the wind.

"I pray to you, O bulls of the holy sites!" she jabbered in dialect. "Jesus, Joseph, and Mary, drive the fire away!"

"Vat's de olt lady doingk?" Hoffer asked in amazement.

"Nothing. Those are the papal bulls of the holy places that the friars of Terrasanta sell for money. They're supposed to keep away fire and water."

The engineer gave up seeking further explanation.

"Mamà!" cried Turiddru.

Again the old woman appeared neither to see nor hear him.

"Patre Virga said the theatre was the work of the devil! He said the theatre was straight out of Sodom and Gomorrah! He's a holy man, is Patre Virga! He said there'd be fire, and fire it is!"

Having used up the bull, Gnà Nunzia went back inside. Turiddru noticed that, somehow or other, Hoffer's machine had managed to tame the flames a little. Without a word, he broke into a run, went through the front door, and shot up the stairs.

Not five minutes later, Turiddru Macca emerged from the smoke with Gnà Nunzia draped over his shoulder, immobile.

"Did she faint?" inquired Puglisi.

"No, sir. I punched her in the face."

"Why did you do that?"

"She said she didn't want to come down in her night-gown with all these wicked men about."

"The fire in dis haus ist kaput!" said engineer Hoffer, practically singing for joy. "Who eltz liffs upshtairs?"

Puglisi looked up.

"There's a widow lives on the second floor, Concetta Riguccio. But there's been no sign of her. With all this com-motion at this hour of the night, she would have asked for help if she was at home. I know the lady. She probably went to sleep at her sister's house tonight."

Only the young have such feelings

Only the young have such feelings, thought Don Pippino Mazzaglia with a touch of envy and another of commiseration while listening to the speech of Nando Traquandi, the young man who had arrived from Rome under cover of secrecy and whom he'd been hiding at his country house for the past week. Slender, with reddish, curly hair and small spectacles behind which flashed a pair of wild eyes, the Roman raised his left hand to his chin every now and then to scratch, tic-like, a thin beard, while every four or five words his right hand brought a small handkerchief to his lips to wipe away the little white spot of condensed spittle that formed at each corner of his mouth.

Traquandi had arrived in Sicily with two letters of recommendation, one from Napoleone Colajanni and one from the Honorable Pantano, member of parliament, asking their Mazzinian friends to provide refuge, assistance, and sustenance to the young man, who, they said, had been entrusted with a mission as dangerous as it was secret. Pippino Mazzaglia had obliged him, but from the very first words he exchanged with him, he had formed a precise idea of the whole matter: that nothing but trouble would come of the outsider's presence in Vigàta. The youth saw the light of only one truth: that white was white and black was black. He hadn't lived long enough to understand that when black comes very close to white, close enough to touch it, a middle line forms, a line of shadow, where white is no longer white and black is no longer black. The shade of that line is called gray. And inside that line, where the colors, in marrying, give birth to a third, it is difficult to name things precisely and see them in clear outline. It's like when the evening advances and the darkness, which is not yet complete, not yet night, makes you mistake a person for a tree. But the young man had none of these concerns; it was clear that he knew where to put his feet when the light faded.

What an unpleasant fellow! Mazzaglia said to himself, as the Roman talked on and on. *I feel like I'm seeing myself, thirty years ago, before the Bourbon court, about to take it up the ass with ten years of hard labor. My pride was eating me alive. That must mean that, at the time, I was as big of an asshole as this guy.*

"I have some documents here that show just how extreme the situation has become," the youth said without pausing to catch his breath. "I'm going to read you a few passages from a report to the minister that we managed to get our hands on, though I won't say how."

He adjusted his small eyeglasses, slipped his hand into a satchel full of papers, and started looking. At that moment Nini Prestia, who hadn't taken his eyes off the Roman since they had all gathered there, spoke up for the first time.

"Well, *I'm* certainly not going to ask you *how*, since I don't give a shit *how* you got it."

The young man gave him a confused look, surprised by the violence in those words.

"I didn't quite understand," he said.

"May I ask a question that has nothing to do with anything you've been saying?"

Traquandi's eyes narrowed to two slits. Realizing he had better be on his guard, he automatically responded in Roman dialect.

"If it's got nothing to do with anything, why ask it?"

"Because I feel like it."

"Well, then, go ahead."

"There are four of us here, not counting you, sitting around this table. Pippino Mazzaglia, me, Cosimo Bellofiore, and Decu Garzìa. If you were to find out, let's say, that one of us was planning to report you to the police, what's the first thing you would do?"

"I'd shoot him in the mouth," Traquandi said without hesitation.

"Without even asking why?"

"What the hell do I care why? That's his damn business. But, pardon my asking, why did you want to know?"

"Never mind; it doesn't matter."

~~~

Pippino Mazzaglia felt a surge of heat in his chest so strong and intense that it brought tears to his eyes. There was Ninì Prestìa, forever his true friend, the person with whom he could always wear his heart on his sleeve, who had shared with him more than thirty years of fear, persecution, escapes, ambushes, prison, and rare moments of joy. He remembered the touch of Ninì's warm hand on his own as the Bourbon judges read out the sentence and cut the roots out from under their youth, cancelling all the books they might read, words they might say, women they might love, children they might caress. And now Ninì had expressed the same feelings as his about the young Roman, as if he had said them out loud. Mazzaglia looked at his friend, keeping his eyes half closed so as not to let any tears show. Ninì had grown old, his hair white, his eye slightly milky. In a flash he realized he was, in a way, looking at himself in the mirror. And so he grew angry, and took Prestìa's side.

"Please bear with us another minute, Signor Traquandi, because I myself would like to ask you something, since you seem to know everything."

The Roman outsider took his hands out of his satchel, laid them on the table, and, without a word, assumed the position of someone ready to listen. But he did it with condescension, and Mazzaglia's antipathy towards him increased.

"What I want to ask you is not simply a waste of time, as you might be inclined to think. Ever since this whole business over *The Brewer of Preston* began, I've been losing sleep asking myself why the prefect of Montelusa got it in his head to inaugurate the Vigàta theatre with an opera that nobody wanted. I found out there's no monetary interest involved, that the composer is not a relative of his, and that he's not sleeping with one of the sopranos. So why, then, did he do it? In order to get the results he wanted, he forced two of the theatre's administrative councils to resign until he found the right sheep to go baaahhh in tempo at the wave of his baton. Why?"

"I couldn't care less why."

"No, I'm sorry, but if this whole business is supposed to provide us with a pretext for staging a demonstration of protest, surely we need to know the real motives of our adversary."

"In that case, I say the prefect wanted to make a show of his own power, and, indirectly, to demonstrate how powerful the government he represents is."

"That's too easy."

"You see? If you keep asking yourself why this and why that, you end up immobilized and unable to act. The truth is that any attempt to understand the adversary is a negotiation with the adversary himself. Talking, discussing, understanding, that's all stuff for—"

"For old folks?"

"I'm sorry, but that's the way I see it."

He lowered his head, pulled a sheet of paper out of his satchel, and showed it to the others.

"This is a secret report from Palermo police commissioner Albanese to Minister of the Interior Medici. These are therefore the words of a fierce adversary of ours."

"No," said Ninì Prestìa, simply and succinctly, still staring at Traquandi, keeping him in his sights.

"What do you mean, 'no'?"

"I mean that *my* fierce adversaries, as you call them, are not people like Albanese, because Albanese is not part of the human race but part of the shit that the human race produces each day."

"Explain yourself."

"Let me give an example, my good friend. Four years after the Bourbons' hangman Maniscalco—with whom my dear friend Pippino Mazzaglia and I had various dealings—went off to Marseille to croak, his wife had the gall to ask the Italian government for a pension. The Accounting Office requested some information from Isidoro La Lumia, director of the Sicilian archives. La Lumia, who was an honest man, began his reply as follows: 'I, the undersigned, am honored to convey the following information concerning the wicked scoundrel who went by the name of Salvatore Maniscalco, and who for ten years was the scourge of Sicily.' So wrote La Lumia. But on that occasion, your enemy, my fine young Roman—Police Commissioner Albanese, that is—took care to make it known that he was not of the same opinion as Don Isidoro. 'The widow should get her pension,' he wrote, 'because'—and I'm not changing so much as a comma— 'because Maniscalco, aside from his excesses, which were justified by circumstance, and aside from the misdeeds he committed by the bushel, had nevertheless been a loyal servant of the state,' and it didn't matter which state. Understand? Two turds, even when shat by different anuses, still have the same smell, and sooner or later end up understanding each other."

"That's fine with me, my friend. So, what should I do, not read it?"

"No, no, go ahead and read it," Mazzaglia said curtly.

"I'll skip around as I read. 'The public spirit in general'— these are Albanese's words—'and particularly in Palermo, is hostile to the government—there is no point in deluding ourselves—or at least accuses those in the government of levying heavy taxes, creating financial disorder, and preventing any growth of industry or commerce.'"

He paused, wiped his lips with his handkerchief, adjusted his spectacles, and continued.

"'Not a single new industry'—this is still Albanese speaking—'has been developed or has created any demand for labor, nor have any large-scale public works provided any bread to workers. And the problem here is mostly bread and jobs. People are beginning to think that the cause may lie not in single individuals but in the institutions themselves; whence it follows that while, on the one hand, the enemies of the monarchy are sharpening their knives and the Mazzinian federalists are thinking of federalism and regional government, there is no lack of people calling for dictatorship. And more new taxes will generate still more discontent.'"

Having finished reading from the document, he put it carefully back inside his satchel and pulled out another.

"This instead is a report from the commanding officer at Caltanissetta. He writes as follows: 'Everyone in this land places his hopes in the anarchy that would follow the momentary triumph of the Mazzinian and socialist sects.'"

"What I would like to know—" said Cosimo Bellofiore, who until that point of the meeting had been completely silent.

"Just another minute," the Roman silenced him, already brandishing another document, "while I read a statement by the prefect of Montelusa, and I quote: 'The discontent has now reached its peak. It has permeated every level of the citizenry, because no advantage, after more than a decade, has come of the many, very exacting sacrifices that Sicily has suffered for the sake of the unity of Italy, unless one excepts the moral and abstract gain of becoming part of a great nation—meagre consolation for those who have no more bread to appease their own or their families' hunger.'"

He put the document back, removed his spectacles, and ran a hand over his eyelids.

"I'm done, but I could go on and keep citing the words of our enemies, which are exactly the same words we might ourselves use. Let's make no mistake: Italy is a volcano ready to explode. And they know it and are scared. They put our comrades in jail, they find our weapons caches, they confiscate them or burn them up, but the next day new ones crop up, as many as were destroyed. And if we Mazzinians, here in Vigàta, don't take advantage of the opportunity provided us tonight, we're fools."

"What opportunity?" asked Cosimo.

"The opportunity we were given tonight, one hour ago, just as I said. When the people of Vigàta revolted against the prefect."

"Some revolt!" said Mazzaglia. "That was just an act of spite by certain people, a momentary thing."

"Anyway, 'the people,' as you call them, stayed home," added Prestìa. "They didn't go to the opera. The folks attending the opera were professionals, merchants, boat owners. The people, the ones who work in earnest, had already gone to bed."

"You may well be right. But we must take advantage of the situation, make it bigger, make it irreparable. Let me explain. If things are left as they are, you can say all you want, but two days from now it will all be forgotten by everyone. But if we make this thing really big, everyone will be forced to talk about it, and not only here in Vigàta. Do you see what I mean? It has to become a national incident."

"How?" asked Decu Garzìa, suddenly attentive. Any time there was trouble to be made, he was always ready to rush to the front of the line, even if he didn't give a damn why the trouble had arisen in the first place.

Traquandi wiped his lips and looked at each of them, one by one.

"We're going to burn down the theatre."

Mazzaglia jumped out of his chair.

"Are you joking? Anyway, look, the wind is blowing hard tonight, even assuming we were in agreement about burning down the theatre."

"What do you mean, the wind is blowing?"

"The flames could spread to other buildings, where people are sleeping."

"What the fuck do I care who's sleeping? If somebody has to die, so much the better. It'll create an even bigger stir."

You know how I feel about this

"Y̶ou know how I feel about this," Prefect Bortuzzi said sternly, frowning and leaning against the high back of his armchair. He was displeased with the back-and-forth discussion he had been having for the past half hour with his interlocutor, who, courteously but firmly, hadn't budged a millimeter from his position.

What do you expect from a Piedmontese? thought Bortuzzi. *Piemontese falso e cortese,* as the saying went.

"And you, likewise, know how *I* feel about it," brutally replied Colonel Aymone Vidusso, commanding officer of the Royal Forces at Montelusa, looking Bortuzzi straight in the eye, and adding: "I find what is happening utterly senseless."

"Senseless?"

"Yes indeed, sir."

"And why is that?"

"We cannot risk provoking a popular uprising simply because you insist on indulging your whim of staging an opera that, to judge by appearances, the people of Vigàta really do not like and will not tolerate."

"That's not true."

"What's not true?"

"That the people of Vigàta don't like it. The people of

Vigàta don't understand a bloody thing about anything, so
you han imagine how much they know about music. The
fact is that someone, and I don't yet know who, has told them
to behave in this manner."

"And what would be the reason for this?"

"It's very simple, my dear holonel. To oppose, at all costs,
the will of the national government's representative."

"That may be so, Your Excellency. But by insisting, you
risk creating ill will at a moment when it's the last thing we
need, as you should know better than I. I needn't remind you
that this island is a powder keg, and if it hasn't yet exploded,
it is only thanks to the prudence—or, if you prefer, the
fears—of Mazzini. I, therefore, will not put the army, will
not put my men, in the service of obstinacy and pigheaded
behavior."

"On the part of the Vigatese."

"Yes, but on your part as well."

"On *my* part? How dare you!"

Aymone Vidusso miraculously managed to restrain his
urge to punch the prefect in the face.

"Excellency, let us try to remain calm and speak reasonably."

"Oh, I am very reasonable, you know. And I say, huite
reasonably, that when there is a danger of unrest against the
instituted authority, the state, all the armed forces—all of them,
I say, regardless of branch or service—must, by God, be united
in the will to put down the uprising, without splitting hairs.
These Sicilians smell bad, do you know that or don't you?"

The colonel made no sign of having heard him. He did
not answer the question, but merely adjusted his monocle.

"Well, they do," Bortuzzi persisted. "They smell bad,
and the Vigatese even worse than the rest."

"I'll not enter into the subject of odors," the colonel said diplomatically. Indeed, to him, it was His Excellency himself, the prefect, who had for some time already begun to smell bad. "But let me reiterate that it has never been, to my knowledge, legitimate to force anyone to enjoy an opera by means of prefectorial decree."

As soon as he said these words, he froze and fell silent in amazement. Where on earth had he, the unbending Piedmontese, come up with a statement so ironic? Apparently the prefect was getting on his nerves as never before. He collected himself and continued.

"If you wish to do so, of course, you may. But you are not free to do so. And it's quite possible that someone will see your actions as an abuse of power. That is your affair. The Italian army, however, cannot and must not be implicated in so foolish a scheme. And I will, in any case, ask the opinion of the proper authorities. Now, if you'll excuse me."

He rose, tall and stiff, wedged his monocle more firmly in his eye, brought his hand to his visor, and executed a half bow. Bortuzzi darkened as he watched the maneuver. His eyes would have burnt the colonel if they could.

"Holonel," he said. "Holonel, I am warning you. I have no choice but to see your actions as an explicit refusal to homply. And thus I shall have to file a report to your immediate superior. That would be General Hasanova, is that not correct?"

"Yes, sir, Avogadro di Casanova. Do as you see fit, Your Excellency."

He turned on his heel and went out, closing the door behind him.

"Nincompoop of a nincompoop!" His Excellency muttered. "You're going to pay for this! You're going to find yourself in the eye of the storm with a blizzard in your face! I'll fill you full of shot like a snipe!"

Bortuzzi could mutter to himself all he wanted, because Colonel Vidusso had already covered his rear. Four days before his meeting with the prefect, he had felt which way the wind was blowing and, anticipating a request for the army to intervene in the event that things should take a bad turn, he had written a full and detailed report to Lieutenant General Avogadro di Casanova, stationed in Palermo, in which he explained the degree to which the prefect was an incompetent and, worse, a buffoon, capable of the worst sorts of buffooneries. Actually, more than a clown, he was an individual who had let his power go to his head and in his exercise of this power had not hesitated to ally himself with a shady character and known mafioso. The damage the man was capable of doing by stubbornly imposing *The Brewer of Preston* on the Vigatese was incalculable.

He had summoned his trusty courier, a fellow Piedmontese, to deliver the letter.

"Take this message to the commander. I want you to hand it personally to General Casanova. And I want an answer by this evening. Think you can manage?"

"Of course I can manage!" said the messenger, offended by his superior's question.

And indeed, at around ten o'clock that evening, the young man returned to Vidusso, covered with mud, eyes beaming with contentment. He handed the colonel an envelope. Curiously, there was no letterhead or seal on the envelope, nor on the letter inside, which looked perfectly ordinary. The message consisted of two lines signed with the unmistakeable initials of General Casanova. It was in Piedmontese:

"*Ca y disa al sur Prefet, cun bel deuit y'm racumandu, c'a vada pieslu 'nt cul.*"

Which, in no uncertain terms, meant:

"You must tell your prefect, tactfully and in accordance with the proper protocol, to go get buggered."

He wasn't sure how tactfully he had done so, but following the general's orders and his own personal inclination, he had indeed told His Excellency to do precisely this.

∿

From the moment Vidusso walked out, the prefect had been sitting with his head in his hands, sputtering curses that grew more and more elaborate as he invented them. He looked darkly at Emanuele Ferraguto, who was entering the office smiling from ear to ear.

"Things don't look so good, Ferraguto. I missed the mark with Vidusso. He's unwilling."

"What happened, Your Excellency?" asked Don Memè, concerned.

"I don't know what to do. That twit Vidusso told me in no uncertain terms that the army, if needed, would not intervene."

"But we don't give a good goddamn, sir."

"You think so?"

"Of course, Your Excellency. We've got Captain Villaroel and his mounted militia, which is more than enough. How much trouble do you think a small handful of beggars from Vigàta can make? Villaroel will keep them in line."

"The point is not how much trouble they might make, Ferraguto. We've got to prevent them from mahing any trouble at all! And, anyway, if anything were to happen, the

intervention of the army would have loohed a bit a less—
how shall I say?—a bit less *private*. Instead, that shit Vidusso
thumbed his nose at me!"

"Excellency, you just keep cool as a cucumber. You have
the solemn word of Emanuele Ferraguto that, when *The
Brewer of Preston* is performed in Vigàta, nothing whatsoever
will happen. Captain Villaroel himself and his twenty-four
horsemen will have all the leisure to stroke their monkeys—
if you'll forgive the expression, Your Excellency—before,
during, and after the music. They'll have nothing to do! So
forget about it and listen up, 'cause I've brought you something wonderful."

From his pocket he extracted a large sheet of paper folded
in eight, smoothed it out, and set it down on the table in
front of the prefect.

"There we are, freshly printed. Be careful not to dirty
your hands with the ink."

It was a copy of *The Guinea Hen*, a satirical weekly printed
out of Montelusa and consisting of a single page that was
constantly raking the prefect's policies over the coals. Don
Memè jabbed his forefinger at a lead article, just under the
masthead, that bore the eye-catching title of "Serious Letter
to the People of Vigàta."

Bortuzzi fell to it avidly.

~~~

The open letter said in essence that "this time it behooves the
people of Vigàta to be courteous" and to heed, for once, the
words of a Montelusan periodical. The author of the article,
who was the editor in chief himself, Micio Cigna, knew well
"how the Vigatese, at every possible opportunity, have always

scorned the advice and exhortations so generously offered from their administrative capital of Montelusa towards the laudable goal of civic progress in the subsidiary port of Vigàta." Concerning the matter in question in the article, however, Micio Cigna begged them please to pay due attention. It was widely known that, for the imminent inauguration of the new theatre of Vigàta, it had been decided by a majority, "after protracted discussion that became quite heated at moments and saw honest and worthy men attacking one another, though always for the common and agreed purpose of offering the citizenry the best that could be had in the always debatable field of art," to present a musical opera unfortunately not known and appreciated by all: *The Brewer of Preston*, by Luigi Ricci, which "has enjoyed great success in other theatres across Italy." After the announcement of this choice for the inaugural performance, Micio Cigna continued, "unusual antagonisms, rancorous whisperings, and scarcely repressed incitements to outright rejection were stirred up in order to achieve partisan ends." The author in no way wished to go into "the reasons for this animosity," much less provide an analysis of the "lofty merits of the opera itself"; he merely wanted to appeal to the "intelligence and civility" of the Vigatese, that they might judge the "true worth" of the opera only after "said work" had been performed.

Micio Cigna was asking nothing more than this of the people of Vigàta: a judgment that was "just, though it be harsh," as the Vigatese had had ample opportunity to demonstrate on other, "much weightier" matters.

The open letter concluded as follows:

"Prejudice has always done far greater harm, and led to much harsher misfortune, than wise and well-informed judgment, however negative, would have done in such instances."

✈

After reading the piece, His Excellency's face brightened a little. Don Memè's smile grew even broader.

"Well, thank goodness for that," said the prefect. "For once this *Guinea Hen*, which has brohen my balls so many times in the past, has done the right thing. And you know something, Ferraguto? I wasn't expecting it. Was it you who made them see reason?"

"It didn't take much, Your Excellency. Don Micio Cigna is a man who knows how to use his brains."

"This article will be a big help. Thank you, Ferraguto."

It was a well-known fact that, with Micio Cigna, there was never any point in trying to reason face-to-face. When he got an idea in his thick Calabrian head, he dug in his heels, and there was no way in heaven or on earth to make him change his mind. Wise to his intentions—namely, that *The Guinea Hen* was going to publish an article inviting the Vigatese to piss on the opera, the singers, and the prefect along with them—Don Memè had made the first move, not wasting any time or words. Micio Cigna happened to be engaged to the daughter of Don Gerlando Curtò, and they were to marry within the year. Six days before the planned publication of the article against *The Brewer of Preston*, a thousand head of sheep belonging to Don Gerlando were poached during the night by masked individuals who had clubbed the guardians silly. And although Don Gerlando did his best to open the gates of hell, nary a hair of any of his sheep had turned up. Two days before the article was to appear, Don

Gerlando was paid a visit by a ceremonious, unctuous, smiling Don Memè.

"Don Gerlando, I want you to know that I've taken the liberty of recovering your sheep myself."

Curtò showed no joy at this news; on the contrary, he grew worried. What would Don Memè request in return? For it was clear to him that the person claiming to have found his sheep was the very man who had shanghaied them in the first place. He said nothing, and Don Memè continued.

"I couldn't allow for a man as upright and esteemed as yourself to be wronged that way."

"Do you know who did it?"

"Outsiders, people who don't know our way of doing things."

"Thank you," Don Gerlando was forced to say, through clenched teeth.

"Just doing what's right. Your sheep are in the Inficherna district. Two friends of mine are looking after them now. Just send someone for them when you want them back. And rest assured that you won't have to suffer this sort of affront ever again."

"Tell me what I can do to return the favor."

Don Memè suddenly put his hand over his heart, as if he had been shot there, and twisted his face up in pain.

"Do you really want to offend me?"

"No offense intended, Don Memè. But I, too, want to do what's right."

"Well, okay. But it's just a silly little thing. I want you to say two words to your future son-in-law, who seems to me a rather reckless person, someone who could do a lot of harm."

"I'm at your service."

"It's the humblest of requests."

And Don Memè explained to Curtò what he should say to Micio Cigna.

The shouts exchanged between the future father-in-law and son-in-law kept the neighbors up all night.

"If you don't do what I say, the most you'll ever see of my daughter is through a telescope!"

"Who do you think you are to give me orders? I write what I want to write and what I feel like writing."

The commotion subsided at the first light of dawn. The upshot was an article that His Excellency read with obvious satisfaction.

The early morning sun hung milky and wan

The early morning sun hung milky and wan behind layers of cloud, as if it didn't feel much like rising over Vigàta that day. Hanging in the air was a stale, dark-brown smell tending to black. This penchant for giving odor a color was a quirk of Lieutenant Puglisi. Once, when he told the police commissioner during a stakeout that he was struck by a yellow smell of mown wheat, his superior very nearly had him shipped off to a madhouse.

The theatre was still burning, making more smoke than fire, but only inside its perimeter. The outer walls had withstood the blaze even though the roof had collapsed and was slowly smoldering inside that giant sort of furnace. Engineer Hoffer and his exhausted men continued to spray water with their machine, their reprovisioning now coming from ten or so large barrels transported by five wagons made available to them by Commendator Restuccia. The commendatore had, of course, been one of the plotters against the opera, but he had felt indignant about the fire—a case of arson, in his opinion. And so he'd decided to help the engineer out. The loading and unloading of the barrels was being handled by the militiamen, who had nothing left to do, since most of the population had gone home to bed a good while earlier.

Puglisi couldn't resist the temptation to follow their example, but out of a sense of duty he decided upon a middle course. His flesh felt heavy, his bones ached, his head was in a fog, but what made him feel worst of all was the sensation of dirt and scum on his skin, caused by the smoke and the mud. He thought he could at least allow himself a bath and then come back to keep an eye on operations. The most he would lose was half an hour.

"You wait here," he said to a uniformed policeman he had posted as guard in front of the half-burnt building in which Gnà Nunzia and the Pizzutos lived, to prevent the usual bastards from going inside and looting. "I'll be back in a bit. As long as it takes me to go home and bathe."

He turned to go to the place he called home: two rooms with a latrine and the use of a kitchen, which he rented from Signora Gesualda Contino, a septuagenarian who treated him like a son.

Ruin and desolation reigned in the piazza in front of the theatre, which the mayor had chosen to embellish with a small garden and a single file of oil lamps arrayed in a circle. All the damage had been done before the fire broke out, by the mounted soldiers' horses and the fleeing crowd of frightened people. The garden hardly existed anymore, and three of the six lampposts lay on the ground, uprooted. At the far end of the square was a smashed-up carriage with its wheels in the air, while another lay next to it on its side, with the dead horse still attached. Puglisi looked towards the façade of the theatre, now blackened by smoke. Hoffer's men were entering through the main doorway to go and fight the remaining fire deep in its bowels.

Some discrepancy, some difference, some thing that

didn't tally, slowly worked its way into Puglisi's head. With aching legs, he turned back towards the rear of the theatre, and as he drew near, keeping close to the wall, the signs of the devastation became more and more evident. At last he arrived in the alley behind the building, between the theatre and Gnà Nunzia's house. The guard he had posted saw him reappear.

"Didn't you go home?"

"Not yet. Something occurred to me."

"What is it, sir?"

"It occurred to me I need a breath of air, all right?" was his brusque reply. Puglisi liked to ask questions, not to answer them.

He carefully studied the rear façade of the theatre. At street level there were six transom windows, the kind that are hinged at the bottom and serve to allow air and a bit of light into the rooms below, in the basement.

Stumps of frames without panes, eaten up by the fire, were all that was left of them. In the middle of the row of transom windows was a wooden door, or the charred remains of one. Behind it were six stone stairs leading down to the understage. On either side and above the door were the signs of a furious, all-devouring fire much fiercer than in other parts of the theatre. Puglisi stopped in front of the door, bewildered. Then he noticed that the first transom window on the right had by some miracle been almost spared. He went up to it and crouched down to have a better look. The pane had been shattered, but the shards had fallen inwards. Puglisi stood up again and backpedaled slowly until he was up against Gnà Nunzia's building. The overall view confirmed the opinion he was forming: that the fire had not been started when some spectator dropped a still-burning cigar too close to a curtain in the entrance lobby, where the box office and the grand staircase leading up to the boxes, the orchestra, and the gallery were. Its point of origin was on the opposite side of the building.

And the culprit may have been a stagehand who had perhaps gone down to the understage for a smoke. But then why break the panes of the transom windows and leave the door open? There was no doubt, in fact, that the back door had been open at the moment the fire first caught, as one could tell by the remains of the door still attached to its hinges. So why was the door left wide open, creating a strong draft to fuel the fire? Like a Sicilian greyhound, Puglisi came to attention, pricked his ears, and sniffed the air, but his fatigue was so great that he decided to go and get cleaned up first, after which he could study the matter with a lighter, freer head.

∿

It was not his fate, however, to bathe that morning. As he was putting the key in his front door, a question paralyzed him: What made him so sure that the widow Lo Russo, who lived on the floor above Gnà Nunzia, had gone to sleep at the home of her sister Agatina? For the entire duration of the fire and the ensuing pandemonium, she had given no sign of being at home, it was true, but perhaps she hadn't been well and was still there, unconscious or injured, and in need of help. He put the key back in his pocket and stood on the landing a little while longer, trying to decide what he should do: break down the door of the widow's apartment, or go to her sister's place and ask if Signora Concetta had spent the night there.

He opted for the latter course of action, perhaps because he had always, since the first time they met, felt attracted to Agatina Riguccio, wife of Totò Pennìca, a fisherman by trade. And to think that, on that occasion, he had even seen her in unflattering circumstances, after her husband had broken her cheekbone with a punch during a jealous spat—the jealousy being Totò's, of course.

Summoned by the neighbors, Lieutenant Puglisi had found this Agatina with a swollen face but a pair of dark, lively eyes that looked like they were always asking for something, quivering red-violet lips (which smelled of saffron and cinnamon, Puglisi thought), and light, dancing tits under her unlaced bodice.

"Who called you here?" she had said. "There's no quarrel. I slipped and fell and hit my face against the armoire."

"So why were you screaming?"

"Don't you scream, sir, when you hurt yourself?"

Not only beautiful, but shrewd. Six months later, another call. This time she had a nasty purple mark around her neck.

"This? This mark here? But what kinds of ideas are you getting in your head, Lieutenant! I did that myself, when my scarf got caught in a door handle."

But she looked him straight in the eye as she said those words, and there was, in that look, an entirely different question, one that sent shivers down his spine.

"So I can leave without having to worry about you?"

"Of course, Lieutenant. And thanks," and she grabbed his hand to say good-bye.

The way she squeezed it took him by surprise. It was as if she had enveloped his fingers not only with her hand but with her whole body—as if the man's hand, having become something else, had entered her innermost part, all the way to her womanly core.

～～～

He had to knock three times before a sleepy Agatina answered.

"Who's there?"

"It's me, Lieutenant Puglisi."

The door opened in a flash. Agatina stood before him in a nightgown, her skin fragrant with the warm scent of the bed, and the color that immediately suggested itself to Puglisi's senses was the quivering pink of a sea urchin just opened.

"What is it? What's happened? Has something happened to my husband?"

"No, don't worry. Nothing's happened to your husband."

Agatina seemed relieved, as her tits rose and then fell in a long sigh.

"Please come inside."

Puglisi went in, letting himself be lulled by the color of cracked-open sea urchin, which had intensified.

"So what is it?"

"Did your sister Concetta sleep here tonight?"

"No, sir. Why?"

Puglisi shuddered. If she was at home, why hadn't she called for help?

"Have you got a key to her apartment?"

"Yessir."

She went over to a chest of drawers, opened a drawer carefully so as not to wake her three-year-old son, who was sleeping in the double bed, took out a key, and handed it to him. Then she began to tremble.

"What happened, Lieutenant?"

"Didn't you hear anything tonight?"

"No, nothing. We're practically out in the country here. Yesterday evening we went to bed around seven, right after the Angelus bell. Then this morning my husband got up before daybreak to go out on his *paranza*. But what happened? Don't try to scare me!"

She staggered and, to avoid falling, leaned hard on him. Instinctively, Puglisi put his arm around her waist. Upon contact, she strengthened her grip on him. The constable felt slightly dizzy. This woman was very dangerous; he had to get out of there at once.

"Let's do this. Do you have a neighbor here whom you could ask to watch over the kid?"

"Yessir."

"All right, then, after you've arranged that, come and meet me at your sister's place. But listen carefully: you mustn't make any noise or cry out in any way about what you happen to see."

"But what is there to see?"

"There was a fire last night."

"All right," said Agatina, as though resigned.

~~~

Less than ten minutes later, having run all the way back, Puglisi was standing again in front of the man he had posted outside the burnt building. The guard gave him a puzzled look.

"Why, you look rather dirtier and greasier than before, sir."

"Don't give me any shit and don't be a wise guy. Have you heard any voices inside the building?"

"No. Who would be talking in there? Gnà Nunzia went to her son's place and the Pizzutos are in the hospital."

"Listen, I'm going up there, to the top floor."

"Why? The top floor didn't burn. If there was anybody there, they'd already be out by now."

"I didn't ask you your opinion."

The guard fell silent. It was unlike Puglisi to be so rude; it must mean there was something serious afoot.

"In a short while a woman is supposed to come here. Let her inside, but tell her to keep close to the wall when she climbs the stairs. It's less dangerous that way."

As he was going up, he suddenly started taking three steps at a time, but had to move carefully because the staircase didn't inspire much confidence.

The door to the widow's apartment, once green, was now brown from the smoke. He opened it and entered a small black anteroom, black because everything inside the flat had turned black. Taking a few more steps, he found himself in the bedroom. He couldn't see a thing; the smell had turned the color of pitch. A shaft of dim light entered the room through the shutters of the French door, which had been left ajar. He went up to it and flung it open. The light burst in, and the first thing he saw were two ebony statues, life-size, on the bed. They represented the naked bodies of a man and a woman, closely entwined.

Late as usual

"Late as usual, always late," Angelica Gammacurta hissed at her husband as he sat down beside her after inconveniencing, upon his return from the lobby, the four people between the aisle and his seat.

The second act had already begun.

"Act Two started some time ago," Signora Gammacurta declared angrily. "Do you think that's a civilized way to behave, the way you do?"

"I really don't give a damn. Anyway, what's the prefect going to do, call me in for a talk tomorrow, like at school? It's already a lot for me to have come to this tremendous bore of a theatre. Do the other people in the audience look like they're paying closer attention than I am?"

Indeed, the moment he had reentered the auditorium, Dr. Gammacurta thought he was at the fish market the day after the *paranzas'* return, laden with catch. In the orchestra as in the gallery, people were talking aloud about their personal matters, blithely indifferent to what was happening on the stage, where the singers were losing their voices trying to make themselves heard above the great buzz of the audience.

"What was that? I couldn't hear! Would you tell me what he said?" a lady in the second row of boxes asked a man down in the orchestra. "What did Don Simone say? Are you talking about Simone Alfano?"

And the man in the orchestra, half standing, shouted:

"Yes, indeed, Don Simone Alfano. And he said," the man repeated, referring to what an old man sitting five rows up had said, and serving as his spokesman, "that his grandson Tanino cut his finger at the sawmill."

It was all one big commiseration over bereavements and misfortunes, and a cascade of congratulations over marriages, births, and betrothals. Unusually united for once, the towns-folk, uninterested in the opera, had taken advantage of the occasion to trade gossip and news. Gammacurta thus learned, for example, that the price of almonds, like that of fava beans, was going up, whereas that of wheat was on its way down; that sulfur was stable; that the ship carrying salt that was sup-posed to arrive from France was running late due to bad weather encountered around Corsica; that Signora Tabbìsi had finally given birth to a much-desired baby boy; that the wife of Salomone the agronomist had been cuckolding him for the past month; that the Vincis' eldest daughter was unequivocally a slut; that Captain Cumella had been called to God's side and that everyone agreed that God had hesi-tated a bit too long before calling him.

In the royal box, which fell to him in the absence of the king, Prefect Bortuzzi was as white as chalk, while his wife had turned as red as a chile pepper. Mayor Bennici, for his part, was yellow verging on yellow-green. The only people who were the right color appeared to be Don Memè Ferra-guto, with his dangerously broad smile, and the captain of the mounted militiamen, Liborio Villaroel, a stinking bas-tard not only in the eyes of God and his fellow men, but also in those of worms. Bortuzzi squirmed in his gilded armchair—which bore the coat of arms of the House of Savoy—as if he had a hot coal up his ass. He kept turning his head to the left and to the right, waving his hands like the vanes of a windmill, speaking uninterruptedly with the mafioso one minute and with the uniformed representative of the law the next. Everything was going wrong for His Excellency, but not because those openly against the opera were cutting in with goatherds' whistles and noises ranging from cackles to raspberries. Things were bad because *The Brewer of Preston* was being greeted with unanimous indifference. He looked over at Don Memè, who threw up his hands. Against ten people, he might be able to do something. But against a whole town?

◢◣◢◣◢

Once he'd settled into his seat, Dr. Gammacurta decided to focus a bit of his attention on what was happening onstage.

The scene had changed and now displayed the outside wall of a country inn, in front of which were some small tables, chairs, and benches. In the background was a painted landscape with a military encampment, and, indeed, a number of officers and soldiers stood in front of the door to the inn, singing.

"Who are they?" the doctor asked his wife.

"They're English soldiers."

"I can see that. I mean, what are they doing there?"

"They're looking for the brewer's twin brother. This brother had something going with a certain Anne, the sister of a ship's captain, but then he ran away. I think there's going to be a mistake."

"What do you mean?"

"A case of mistaken identity. The soldiers looking for the twin will arrest the brewer, thinking he's his brother."

A mistake. If the plot went the way his silly wife Angelica thought, the opera would never have any chance of success. How many things, in Sicily, happened by mistake, compared with those that happened without mistakes as to the identities of people and things? In Vigàta alone, and keeping only to the past three months, Artemidoro Lisca was murdered on a moonless night when he was mistaken for Nirino Contrera; Turiddruzzu Morello married Filippa Mancuso by mistake after deflowering her one night without realizing that she was not her sister Lucia, who had been the one foreordained; Pino Sciacchitano died because his wife mistook rat poison for the tonic her husband took after every meal. And suspicions in the end arose that all these mistakes were actually phony mistakes, not mistakes at all, but only alibis, even deliberate acts. So how were people supposed to laugh at a mistake more phony than real phony mistakes, when they lived in a world of daily mistakes?

After this reflection, Dr. Gammacurta went back to watching the action on the stage, which involved a certain Tobias, Daniel the brewer, and his fiancée, Effy.

This Tobias was trying to teach Daniel how to look like a proper military man, with the stiff carriage of someone who has swallowed a broomstick, the head as though in the same plaster cast as the neck, and the gait of someone with wooden legs. Tobias imitated the sound of snare drums with his voice, *rat-a-tat*, *rat-a-tat*, but Daniel seemed unable to learn, whereas his fiancée, Effy, for her part had no problem marching in step, being more man than woman. It came naturally to her. Tobias was delighted at Effy's ability:

"She learned it all in a moment,
like a soldier of the regiment."

Then, Gammacurta wondered, momentarily drawn into the story, *it's him, Daniel, who wants to be mistaken for his brother, the military man. But why?*

He turned towards Angelica, who looked hypnotized by what was happening onstage.

"Why does Daniel want to be mistaken for his twin brother?" he asked her.

"I don't know; I don't get it."

"Then why the hell are you watching all bug-eyed as if you were spellbound?"

"The costumes," said Angelica.

Gammacurta felt his stomach turn at that answer. He realized he would never make it to the end of the performance.

"I'm going."

"Where?"

"Where do you think I'm going at this hour of the night? I'm going home."

"Aren't you going to stop first at your medical office?" Angelica asked him with a smirk.

A provocation, to which he promptly reacted.

"No, tonight nobody needs any care. Good-bye."

He roused himself, begging pardon for again disturbing the four people separating him from the aisle and who this time looked at him askance and cursed under their breath. How his wife had figured out that he'd been having an affair with the town's midwife, and that he was lying when he came home from work late saying he had been at the office, the doctor did not yet understand. At least twice a week the fresh thighs and firm tits of Ersilia Locuratolo, the midwife, consoled him for his daily suffering, yet very few people knew about it. Apparently, however, these very few included some cornuto who had told his own wife, who, in turn, had hastened to inform Angelica. But he really did feel tired that night, and wanted only to go to bed, unaccompanied.

He was about to raise the heavy velvet curtain over the orchestra doorway leading into the lobby when a very loud voice rose above the din of audience chatter, the singing of the singers, the music of the orchestra, and stopped him in his tracks.

"*Signor Prefetto! Signor Prefetto!*" the voice called desperately for the prefect from the gallery.

A stunned silence suddenly came over the theatre. Even the singers stood paralyzed, mouths open, as the conductor froze, arms half raised.

"*Signor Prefetto!*" the voice continued. "How am I supposed to react to this scene? Should I laugh? Give me your orders, so I can obey. Let us know what you want, *Signor Prefetto!*"

Gammacurta raised the curtain then let it fall back down behind him, muffling the laughter of the audience and the sounds and voices of the opera, which resumed its *Via Crucis*. He pulled his cloakroom ticket out of his pocket and handed it to the employee.

"Overcoat and hat, please."

The man working in the cloakroom, Ninì Nicosìa, was a patient of his and promptly gave him his garments, smiling.

"How are you feeling, Ninì? Belly still bothering you?"

"No, sir." Then he brought his face close to the doctor's and said slowly, "Be careful, Doctor."

"Careful?" Gammacurta asked in astonishment. "Careful about what?"

"Just be careful, Doctor," the other repeated without explaining.

The doctor put on his overcoat, headed towards the large glass-and-wood entrance door of the theatre, and went out. He hadn't taken three steps before he was stopped by two soldiers armed with carbines.

"Where are you going?" one of them asked in a typical cop-like tone that set Gammacurta's nerves on edge, even though he had never had any problems with the law or its representatives. Thus he answered rudely.

"None of your goddamn business."

"You can't," said the second soldier.

What had got into those two assholes? In the corner of his eye he saw another man in uniform approaching, wearing the rank of lieutenant. The man saluted respectfully, bringing his hand to his visor.

"Please excuse us, sir, but these are His Excellency the prefect's orders. No one is to leave the theatre before the opera is over."

"Is this some kind of joke?" cried Gammacurta.

"No, sir. And you must either return at once to your seat or I shall have to put you in jail. It seems to me hardly worth spending the night in jail for something so silly."

The lieutenant, clearly, didn't want any argument. Bewildered, the doctor turned around and went back inside. Ninì Nicosìa, who had watched the scene from behind the glass, signaled to him to stay calm. But by now a blind rage was making Gammacurta teeter like a tree in a windstorm. There had to be another way out of that goddamn theatre. Driven

by a sort of instinct and determined not to yield to the soldiers' and the prefect's commands, the doctor, instead of
going back into the auditorium and sitting down in his seat
(among other things, the people he kept inconveniencing
would surely have come to blows with him this time), walked
the length of the half-horseshoe-shaped corridor that ran
along that side of the orchestra, found himself in front of a
small door, opened it, and went inside. It gave onto a small
landing with two staircases leading away from it: one went
up to the stage, while the other led down to the understage.
He chose the latter. He couldn't very well barge in on the
singers; it would have triggered another '48. Feeling increasingly in the grips of a blind rage, he wanted to go home, and
go home he would. Suddenly he found himself in a very
large room, dimly lit by a few oil lamps. There were rolled-up
backdrops, cables, rafters, costumes, helmets, barrels, swords.
Near the back wall he saw a closed door. Above him he could
hear the muffled voices and footsteps of the singers onstage.
The door was at the top of six small steps, which he climbed.
Drawing the bolt, he went through the door and found himself outside, in the alley behind the theatre. He smiled. He
had foiled the soldiers and prefect. He tried closing the door
behind him, but could only manage to shut it halfway; something was preventing the hinges from rotating. He left it ajar
and took a few steps. At that moment he heard someone
shout.

"Stop! Thief!"

He looked around, truly scared this time. A mounted
soldier sat motionless on his horse at the corner of the alley,
aiming his carbine at the doctor.

"Put your hands up, thief!"

A mistake. The soldier was convinced he was a thief who had made his way into the understage area to steal things. The doctor smiled, but instead of stopping to explain, he turned and started running, losing his hat as he heard the horse's hooves approaching behind him.

"Stop or I'll shoot!"

He kept running, short-winded, past Gnà Nunzia's house until he found himself behind it, by the large deposit of salt. He resolutely went inside, thinking the soldier's horse wouldn't be able to move through that sea of salt as fine as sand. Indeed the soldier did not enter, but merely stopped his horse, took careful aim at the black shadow that stood out against the whiteness of the salt despite the darkness, and fired.

I wish either my father

"I wish either my father or my mother, or both, had thought twice before letting me be born," Decu Garzìa said very slowly, as if talking to himself. Then he paused, took a breath, and continued.

"I really mean it. In all honesty."

Only the two of them, Traquandi and Garzìa, remained in Pippino Mazzaglia's study. At the suggestion that they should set fire to the theatre, Ninì Prestìa had withdrawn with an indignant expression on his face and was accompanied home by Cosimo Bellofiore, who was of the same firm opinion as he.

Now the two were awaiting the return of Don Pippino, who had gone to get what the young Roman had asked of him. Nando Traquandi seemed interested in what Garzìa was saying, but solely out of simple courtesy towards the only ally he had left.

"Why?"

"Because I myself don't even know what comes over me the moment I hear there's a chance to wreak havoc. Want to burn down the theatre? Then let's burn it down! Decu's ready and able! Want to set the town on fire? Give Garzìa a torch! Want to bugger the whole world? Here I am, first in line! But why? How? For what reason? I just don't care about anything at all. As soon as there's any damage or devastation to be done, any bedlam to sow, I get the itch for it, and I want to be part of it."

"So you're trying to tell me you're going along with me without any real reason, just because you feel like it? That there's no thought behind it, other than wanting to wreak havoc?"

"That's right."

"I gotta tell you something from the heart, my friend: I don't give a damn why you do anything. It's enough for me that you do it."

"Oh, I'll do it, all right, you can bet your balls I'll do it. I didn't say what I just said only to bow out."

Don Pippino came in carrying a tin that stank of kerosene and set it down on the small table along with a short iron rod.

"Will this tin of kerosene be enough?"

"I think so."

"All right, then. Tomorrow morning, I'll send a servant to Decu Garzìa's house with your suitcase and clothes. I don't want you setting foot back here after the deed."

Traquandi stared at him.

"I know you're a brave man," he said, "and therefore you're not chasing me away because you're afraid of the consequences. So why, then? I think I know the reason: you despise me."

"Yes," Mazzaglia said firmly.

"Want to tell me why, or are you just kidding?"

"No, I'm not kidding; this is hardly the time for jokes. Several times, and with increasing frequency, I've seen the Italian army fire at people who were protesting because they were starving to death. They even shot at women and children. And I felt rage and shame. Rage because one can't just sit there, cool and calm, watching innocent people get killed. And shame because I myself, through my words, my actions, my years in prison, my exile, had a hand in creating the Italy that has turned out this way, with one part suffocating the other and shooting it if it rebels. I want to stop feeling ashamed for supporting people like you, who may even see things as I do but have no qualms about spilling other people's blood. And there you have it. End of sermon."

Nando Traquandi got up from his chair without answering, followed by Decu Garzìa.

"Would you happen to have a piece of rope?"

Don Pippino pulled a skein of thick twine out of a drawer, unwound it, and cut off a long piece. Traquandi passed one end through the handle of the kerosene tin, knotted it to the other end, and draped the whole thing across his chest. Heading for the door, he and Garzìa put on their overcoats. Pippino opened the door, looked around, didn't see anyone, then signaled to the other two to go out. The weather outside was still bad.

"Do you need a lamp?"

Garzìa was about to say yes, being afraid to break his neck along the road, which was full of stones and holes, but Traquandi spoke first.

"No, thanks. It's better we go in the dark."

They headed off without saying good-bye to Don Pippino.

〰

They took their first steps in silence, and the night was so dark they risked breaking not only their necks but also their legs in the bargain. They walked on a bit longer with caution, afraid to take a wrong step, then slowly their eyes adjusted to the darkness. The Roman youth asked:

"Anybody here in town sell *dindaroli*?"

"What's that?" asked a puzzled Garzìa.

And to his great astonishment, Nando started speaking in rhyme.

> *"The dindarolo makes a ringing sound;*
> *It's made of fired clay and almost round:*
> *It's empty inside and on top has a button,*
> *and a broad and sturdy base on the bottom.*
> *There's also a slot, right up near the crown,*
> *Where the pennies come raining down*
> *When the kiddies in all their thrift*
> *Save up to buy themselves a gift."*

"I get it," said Decu. "Your *dindarolo* is what we call a *caruso*, the thing that little kids put their spare change in— their pennies, as you called them."

"But doesn't a *caruso* mean a little kid in Sicilian?"

"Yeah, but it also means a piggy bank."

"So where can we find some *dindaroli*?"

"I'll tell you in a second. But first tell me something. Do you write poetry yourself?"

Traquandi gave a tubercular laugh and brought his handkerchief to his mouth.

"I wish, but I'm really not cut out for it. Those lines are by Giuseppe Berneri, a Roman poet who wrote the *Meo Patacca*. He's the one who gave me the idea to set fire to the theatre. Berneri says that whenever the Romans decided to attack the ghetto where the Jews lived, they would take a bunch of *dindaroli*, fill them with gunpowder, stick a wick in the coin slot and light it, then throw them into the Jews' houses. The *dindaroli* would break and the powder would spread all over the place and catch fire. It's a great idea, really."

They fell silent. The trail was treacherously steep, and talking was a distraction.

Swearing, slipping, crashing, falling, teetering, and staggering, they finally left the trail behind them and arrived at a well-beaten road. Nando leaned on an extinguished lamppost for a moment to catch his breath. He was sweating and his eyeglasses had steamed up.

"What's the lighting in town like?" he asked.

Decu answered at once, happy not to have broken any bones during the descent.

"The outlying streets have a few oil lamps like this one, but there are more in the center of town, and they run on kerosene."

"What time do they go on and off?"

"It varies."

"What do you mean?"

"The contract for the town's lighting was given to an uncle of mine, and that's the only reason why I can tell you how it works. In the summer, they keep the lamps on late, since people like to linger and stroll about in the heat, but in the winter, they shut them off earlier."

"Well, it's winter now. What does 'earlier' mean?"

"It depends on how much my uncle and Vanni Scoppola stand to gain. Scoppola's the elected deputy at city hall. I'll explain. Say Scoppola needs money; he goes to my uncle and says: We'll announce that the lights will go out at nine, but you turn them off at seven. And we'll divide those two hours of unused kerosene between us. Do you follow me?"

"Like a light," said Traquandi, smiling at the pun. "And what kind of lighting is there around the theatre?"

"Kerosene."

"Are there fixed lamps? I don't mean in the square in front; there are a ton of them there."

"There are lampposts in front of the two doctors' houses, the midwife's, the mayor's, and Police Lieutenant Puglisi's."

"Mazzaglia told me this copper Puglisi has it in for the prefect, because the prefect had him investigated for allegedly protecting the numbers racket."

"That's true."

"So this Puglisi's someone you can reason with?"

"I didn't make myself clear. It's true the prefect reported him, but it's also true that Puglisi came out of it clean. But that doesn't mean . . ."

"That doesn't mean what?"

"That Puglisi will let it slide if you burn down the theatre. He's still a cop, and a good one. Here, this is Pitrino's house. He's the one that makes ceramics."

Traquandi looked at the structure, which was barely larger than a doghouse.

"But where's he sleep?"

"Where do you think? Inside."

"And where's the stuff he sells?"

"In back."

And, in fact, behind the cottage was a little yard surrounded by a low picket fence. Climbing over it was child's play for Decu. He grabbed two medium-sized piggy banks and showed them to Nando, who said they would do fine. They resumed walking.

"Which is the fixed lamppost closest to the theatre?"

"The one by the midwife's house."

"Let's go."

∿

Before they got there they had to dive behind a horseless carriage when two mounted militiamen passed on patrol. But there was no real danger. Then they came to the lamp by the midwife's house. They stopped at the edge of the cone of light, then ducked inside a doorway. Traquandi filled the two piggy banks with kerosene, pouring the liquid through the slot made for coins, then tore off a piece of his shirt, which he divided in two, sticking one in each slot. Lastly, he drenched the protruding part of each rag in kerosene.

"We can go now," he said.

They advanced very cautiously, as they could hear the soldiers who were still guarding the piazza, even if they couldn't see them. They turned onto a small street parallel to the theatre's side wall and ended up behind the building. Now they couldn't hear or see a living soul.

"Here we are," Traquandi said in a low voice. "You go to the right-hand side. I want you to smash all the panes on those little windows, then throw in the *dindarolo*. I'll do the same on the other side. Wait, let me light it for you."

He set fire to the wick of Garzìa's piggy bank, then lit his own.

"Hurry."

With the iron rod Traquandi shattered the first window-pane, trying to make as little noise as possible. Then he heard Decu's muffled voice.

"Nando, come 'ere, quick."

Traquandi arrived in a flash. Without speaking, Decu

pointed out to him the half-open door leading to the understage.

"Here, gimme your *dindarolo* too," said the Roman. "You, in the meantime, break all the windows; it'll create a draft."

Carrying both piggy banks, smoke rising from their fuses, Traquandi descended the stone staircase until he found himself under the stage. In one corner he noticed four trunks full of costumes, and without hesitation he hurled the first money box against them, shattering it at once. The trunks immediately caught fire. By the brighter light of the first flames, he looked around calmly. In another corner he spotted a great many rolled-up stage backdrops, propped against the wall. Hurled with great force, the second piggy bank turned them into gigantic torches. He raced back up the stairs, out of breath.

"Let's get out of here, fast."

"Where to?"

"Your place, Garzìa. I suddenly feel hungry, and sleepy, too. Got any good wine?"

By now everyone knew him

By now everyone knew him as Don Ciccio, and he, moreover, did not object, despite the fact that his given name was Amabile and his surname Adornato. Amabile Adornato, known as "Don Ciccio." He had come to Vigàta from Palermo some ten years before the events that occurred at the theatre on inauguration night; he had worked there as a carpenter and became known as a master craftsman.

Left a widower, he moved to Vigàta to be closer to his only son, Minicuzzo, who taught elementary school. Since he had made good money practicing his art in Palermo, enabling him to send his Minicuzzo to university, he was able to buy a warehouse in Vigàta—a sort of depository where he could continue to ply his trade—as well as a small house where he could live by himself and not bother his son, who had married in the meantime and had two small children. It took him little or no time to win admiration for his skills not only in Vigàta but also in Montelusa, Fela, and Sfiacca, and thus he never lacked for work.

Don Ciccio had one peculiarity: not only had he studied music and could read it, but he could play the flute as well as the angels were said to play when God Almighty ordered them to perform. After being implored again and again by those who had discovered this peculiar talent of his, he had decided to hold a two-hour music recital, not more, every Sunday afternoon for his few true friends: the postmaster, a fisherman, the captain of the Palermo steamboat that called at the port of Vigàta every Sunday, a peasant who himself could play the flute—the goatherd's Pan flute, that is—and a few others who, chancing to pass by the warehouse where Don Ciccio held the Sunday recitals, felt like listening to music.

There was no doubt, however, that Don Ciccio was a person who, upon careful consideration, gave rise to some questions. And one above all: Where, and how, had he learned to play and understand music so well? Because there was no doubt whatsoever that in matters of music, Don Ciccio was an expert, with profound knowledge of the subject. And yet, when asked a question, he made like a hedgehog, which closes up in a ball the moment you touch it. At best, when he did decide to open his mouth, he would answer with a variety of monosyllables: *yes*, *but*, *if*, or *no*. One day, however, on his seventieth birthday, when his friends threw a party for him and fêted him to the point of getting him drunk, the steamship captain asked him bluntly:

"Don Ciccio, how did it happen?"

And, to everyone's surprise, he explained how it was that music had entered his life and never left. It was a beautiful tale, one that left his listeners wide-eyed and open-mouthed and sounded like one of those stories we tell and retell little children to help them fall asleep. The news then spread, and every now and then someone would ask:

"Don Ciccio, how did it happen?"

And after that first time, Don Ciccio no longer held himself back when telling the story, further embellishing the events, circumstances, people, and things each time he told it. This earned him an epithet, a nickname: Don-Ciccio-How-Did-It-Happen.

One Sunday, a week before the theatre was to be inaugurated, Don Ciccio was about to bring the flute to his lips to start the recital when the entire general staff of the Family and Progress Social Club—from the Marchese Coniglio della Favara and Dr. Gammacurta to the Canon Bonmartino and Headmaster Cozzo—walked in. There were not enough chairs for everyone. Don Ciccio felt moved and honored. He didn't know what to say or do, but merely looked at them with questioning eyes. The marchese, who ranked first among them in nobility and wealth, got to the point without delay.

"Don Ciccio, please excuse us for our invasion, but we are urgently in need of your esteemed opinion."

Don Ciccio, confused, bowed two or three times to those present.

"I'm at your service, gentlemen."

"Don Ciccio, do you know this opera that our prefect in Montelusa wants us at all costs to hear? I believe it's called *The Brewer of Preston*."

"Yes, sir, I heard it about twenty years ago, in Palermo."

"And what did you think of it?"

A tomblike silence ensued. Don Ciccio seemed to be stalling. In that silence, only the marchese had the courage to press him.

"If it's not too much trouble, could you please give us your opinion?"

Don Ciccio bent down slowly, bringing his left hand to

his back, which ached; with his right hand, he picked up a wood shaving, then straightened up again. He held up the scrap for all to see, like a magician, or a priest in church showing the consecrated host.

"That opera is like this," he said.

He squeezed the shaving between his fingers, crumbled it, and tossed the tiny fragments into the air.

"There's your opera; that's how solid it is."

◂◂◂

The following morning Don Memè arrived at the prefecture as fast as a tetherball, raced up the stairs two steps at a time, burst furiously into the waiting room, and, without even bothering to knock, rushed into the prefect's office. Bortuzzi, who had been studying a drawing of the Temple of Concordia through a magnifying glass, was very nearly frightened at the sight of Ferraguto, half of whose face was laughing while the other half frowned.

"*Dio bonino*, Ferraguto, what is happening?"

"What's happening is that that cornuto of a carpenter in Vigàta, Don Ciccio Adornato, doesn't agree. He doesn't like the opera. And he said as much to the members of the social club and is now going around telling everyone."

His Excellency, reassured, only smiled.

"Oh, come now, Ferraguto! A harpenter? You're afraid of what a harpenter is saying? We're hardly in Bethlehem!"

"Excuse me, Your Excellency, but you're mistaken. This carpenter knows a great deal about music. A very great deal. And when he talks about music, people listen. And now they're listening to him like he's the Sibyl of Cumae."

"Oh, really?"

"Yes."

"So what should we do?"

"We've got to get rid of him."

Bortuzzi turned pale, and the ash from the cigar in his hand fell onto his waistcoat.

"*Madonna 'amiciaia*, Ferraguto, what are you saying? I feel abused!"

Don Memè took offense.

"Nobody's trying to abuse you, Excellency."

"Good God, Ferraguto, let's not have any misunderstandings! In my parts, 'abused' means, how shall I say, disoriented. But, man to man, Ferraguto, is it really your habit to resort to such extreme methods?"

"But what are you imagining, sir?"

Ferraguto finally managed to join the smiling half of his face with the frowning half, and the smile prevailed.

"I just meant get rid of him for a little while, in keeping with the law. You, sir, must speak with Captain Villaroel and tell him to do everything I ask him to do, without any argument."

"Well, if that's what you mean, then all right."

"One final request, Your Excellency. How far along is the dossier for the contract to be awarded to Commendator Lumìa?'

Bortuzzi rummaged through the papers on his desk, picked up a file, opened it, studied it, then looked up at Don Memè.

"I remember the hase well, Ferraguto."

"And so?"

"It's a homplihated matter. This Lumìa is hardly entitled to the hontract, you know."

"Your Excellency, let's be frank. Here's how things stand: The mayor of Vigàta had already granted the contract to Lillo Lumìa, who he plays *tresette* and *briscola* with every other day. But then you delayed the settlement, saying there were irregularities. Right?"

"Right."

"Good. Now, I would like to be able to go to Lumìa and say these exact words to him: 'Don Lillo, I have some very good news for you. His honor the prefect told me that he's reconsidering the matter of the contract.' Not one word more or less than that."

Bortuzzi kept staring doubtfully at him. Don Memè decided it was time to lay his ace down on the table.

"Your Excellency, if I can't say that to him, then I can't do what I would like to do, and Don Ciccio the carpenter will keep shitting on the opera and turning the Vigatese against it. Think it over, Excellency. I will only tell Lumìa that you're reconsidering, nothing more. Then, if, fifteen days from now, you decide otherwise than what Don Lillo expects, the opera will have been presented, and that'll be the end of that."

The prefect heaved a long sigh.

"Well, all right. But, please, Ferraguto, be sure to proceed very harefully."

⁂

Touching his hens' bottoms to feel if they were laying eggs was Commendator Lillo Lumìa's favorite pastime, and this, indeed, was what he was doing in the chicken coop of his villa on the hillside above Vigàta when a servant came running up to tell him that '*u zu* Memè had just arrived on horseback and was waiting for him in the courtyard. Lumìa raced out of the chicken coop and rushed with open arms towards Ferraguto, who was dismounting.

"Don Memè! What a sight for sore eyes!"

"Esteemed Commendatore!"

They embraced, then extended their arms to look at each other at a slight distance, smiling happily, then embraced again.

"Don Lillo, I came in person to bring you some good news."

"I don't even want to hear this news unless you first do me the honor of coming into my house, freshening up, and drinking a glass of wine with me."

"Don Lillo, the honor is always mine, and a great one at that," said Don Memè, following the ritual without missing a step. "But I'm in a hurry to leave. I was pleased just to be able to come in person and bring you the good news."

"All right, then, let's hear it," said Don Lillo, throwing his hands up in resignation, since Don Memè could not do him the honor.

"We'll have other opportunities," Don Memè consoled him. "The good news is that this morning I happened, by chance, to speak with the prefect about your bid for that contract. And I put in a good word for you, since the prefect respects my opinions. And, in fact, His Excellency told me to tell you that he's reconsidering the entire matter. He asks merely that you be patient, and everything should work out in your favor."

Lillo Lumìa literally jumped for joy, rubbed his hands together, and confessed:

"I'd lost hope."

"You should never lose hope so long as you've got this

nose butting in for you!" Don Memè reproached him gently, shaking an admonishing finger.

Again they fell into each other's arms. Don Lillo then took the path indicated by the ritual.

"I would never want to offend you, Don Memè, not for any reason in the world, but is there anything that I, in all modesty, could do for you or for any friend of yours?"

"Are we joking, Don Lillo? I need nothing. Honor me always with your friendship; that will be payment enough."

He had used the word *payment*, which meant that Don Lillo was supposed to insist.

"My friendship is eternal, Don Memè, no need even to discuss it. What can I do for you here and now?"

Don Memè's smile turned into a cordial chuckle.

"You're making me remember something. If you're really very keen to do something, you could give me a hand on a silly little matter, a joke I want to play on a friend."

"I'd be delighted. Just tell me what."

Don Memè told him what. Then, just to be safe, he told him again.

At three o'clock that afternoon, as Don Ciccio was reopening his warehouse, a servant from the Lumìa household appeared. Don Lillo, who liked to have fine furniture in his villa, had been a good client many times.

"What can I do for you?"

"Don Lillo wants you to come and pick up a *tanger*."

"*Étagère*," the cabinetmaker corrected him.

"It is what it is. He would like you to come to the house right now; there's no time to lose."

"Come on, what am I, a doctor?"

Two hours later, Don Ciccio, with the help of two of Lumìa's servants, loaded the *étagère* as gingerly as possible onto his cart and brought it to his storehouse. He had explained to Don Lillo that it would take a good two weeks of work, and Don Lillo had given his approval.

~~~

At seven o'clock the following morning, upon opening his storehouse, Don Ciccio was greeted by Lieutenant Pillitteri of the mounted militia and two of his men. Without a word, the bravos slammed him up against the wall as Pillitteri headed straight for the *étagère*. He opened it, removed a small square of wood that hid a secret compartment, stuck his hand inside, felt around, and pulled out two diamond rings and a necklace that Signora Lumìa had reported missing the previous evening. Pillitteri slapped handcuffs on Don Ciccio and made him cross all of Vigàta between the two horsemen.

"I am not a thief! I am not a thief!" Don Ciccio cried in despair and tears, feeling as if he could die of rage and shame.

The wind rose from the west

The wind rose from the west, from Montelusa way—an angry wind upset that it would never manage to sweep away the heavy clouds stagnating over Vigàta. A gust more furious than the rest slightly lifted the heavy plank that the now-dead stranger had used as a bridge between the mountain of salt and the roof of Concetta Lo Russo's building, then dropped it back down on the tiles with a thud. Standing at the French door, Lieutenant Puglisi looked away from the plank and back into the bedroom, and what he saw there disturbed him. The wind had detached the soot from the walls, floor, and every other surface of the bedroom, and a nasty cloud of gray dust floated in the air, giving the impression that the two corpses on the bed had come back to life and were starting to make love again, rocking slowly back and forth. Leaving the shutters open so he could see better, Puglisi closed the great window, and at that moment the wind died down, giving way to a dense, heavy rain that drummed hard on the roof as it bounced off. Puglisi felt cold, and one shudder after another ran down his spine, making him shiver.

A voice began calling him from the staircase. It was Agatina.

"Lieutenant! Lieutenant!"

He raced out of the bedroom, crossed the anteroom in two strides, and stopped on the landing.

"I'm here, Signora Agatina. Come on up, and be very careful on the staircase."

When the young woman got to the top, short of breath, he took her by the hand and brought her into the vestibule. The first thing Agatina did was open her eyes wide and ask:

"Why did she paint the place all black?"

"It hasn't been painted. That's soot from the smoke. And it's toxic."

He wanted to tell her tactfully and cautiously what had happened, but Agatina was sharp and quickly drew the conclusion.

"And where was my sister—in her room?"

"Yes."

"Sleeping?"

"Yes."

It would not have been humanly possible for her to open her eyes wider, yet she did and then opened her mouth to scream. This, however, was exactly what Puglisi by nature couldn't stand: a woman's cries and tears. Violent and sudden, the policeman's slap twisted Agatina's face entirely to one side and sent her crashing against a wall. Puglisi was on top of her at once, his whole body crushing her.

"Be quiet. Don't move, don't shout. Keep still, or I'll give you another whack that'll take your head off. Do you hear me? Keep still or I'll smash your face. Look at me. Do you understand?"

Stunned, she looked at him for a moment, then nodded her head several times to say she understood and wouldn't move.

"Now pay attention. I'm going to take you into the other room to show you what happened, but you mustn't say or do anything."

He turned her around like a lifeless puppet, put her face to the wall, grabbed her from behind by the hips, lifted her into the air, and carried her into the other room. Agatina barely had time to see the two statues on the bed before an unstoppable stream of vomit shot out of her mouth, soiling the constable's shoes. She started muttering meaningless words. Still holding her in midair, Puglisi carried her into the kitchen, sat her down on the only chair at the small table, grabbed a clay pot, dipped it into the water jug, let it fill, then started meticulously washing Agatina's face and mouth.

"Feel better now?"

"Yessir."

"Then listen to me: your sister died happily, in her sleep, after making love. Do you hear me?"

"Yessir."

"She didn't realize she was dying; believe me, she felt no pain or fear. I'm sure of this, because I have experience with these sorts of things."

She seemed to calm down, to the point that she got up from the chair and began washing her face again. But she was trembling all over.

"Who is he? Do you know him?" asked Puglisi.

"He's the Inclimas' boy. The one with only one eye."

"If his eyes had been open, I would have recognized him," said the lieutenant. "His name was Gaspàno Inclima. How long had it been going on?"

"How long had what been going on?"

"How long had they been lovers?"

"They weren't lovers."

"Oh, no? Then how do you explain that your sister and Gaspàno Inclima were in bed together naked and fucking?"

"It must have been the first time, Lieutenant. The first and last."

The first time. The first after five years of strict abstinence as a widow. A bit of happiness, which she paid for with her life.

What kind of bleeding justice is there in the world of God and men? Puglisi asked himself, without opening his mouth.

As if she had read his mind, Agatina echoed his thought.

"What kind of justice is this? First she pays with her life, and now with her honor!"

And this time she started weeping long and disconsolately, which was all the more pitiable as she did it almost silently, without words, without wailing, only a sniffle every now and then.

"What kind of justice is it?" she kept muttering. "And her honor, too?"

Puglisi raised a hand and let it rest on her hair. He kept it there, without hinting at a caress, just to let her know he was there, by her side. Then she straightened up, took his hand into her own, looked at it, saw that it was grimy and black with soot, brought it to her lips, kissed it, looked at it again, brought it again to her lips, and began licking it at length, with care, like a dog. When she had fully cleaned it, she placed it against her cheek and held it there, pressing it with her hand. They remained for a moment in silence, then Puglisi made up his mind.

"You wait here," he said, "and don't move. Even if you hear noises, don't give in to your curiosity. I'll call you when everything's been taken care of."

He went back into the bedroom, approached the two corpses, reached out with one hand, and felt both bodies. They were still soft to the touch; apparently the heat of the soot had retarded rigor mortis. He took off his jacket, trousers, and shirt, and stood there in his woolen undershorts and jersey. He heaved a long sigh and got down to work.

➤➤➤

Less than half an hour later, he returned to the little kitchen and stopped beside Agatina, buttoning his shirt. Then he put his hand under her chin and forced her to look up.

"I've set everything right," he said. "Now be brave and come with me. You must tell everyone what you're about to see; you must say that everything was this way when you first came in."

The woman stood up but then immediately sat back down. Her legs failed her; she couldn't stand up on her own. Grabbing her by the armpits, which felt wet with sweat, Puglisi set her on her feet, turned her around, and pushed her towards the bedroom, forcing Agatina to walk despite the fact that her legs, no longer flaccid, had turned wooden.

"Now look," he said simply, keeping a hand over her mouth, just to be safe.

The scene in the bedroom had completely changed. On the bed lay Concetta, no longer nude but in her slip, looking as if she were sleeping peacefully. The young man, on the other hand, lay stretched out on the floor facedown, fully dressed, feet pointed backward towards the French door, one arm on the bed.

"See him? Try to remember what you see here," Puglisi said with his lips in Agatina's ear. "The lad happened to be passing by when he realized a fire had broken out, and since he couldn't come in through the front door, which was engulfed in flames, he had the presence of mind to enter from behind. He laid down a plank between the mound of salt and the roof, clambered up, leapt onto the balcony, opened the shutters that your sister had left ajar, and entered the bedroom, only to run straight into a thick cloud of smoke. He lost his breath and fell, unfortunately, due to the wind; the window closed behind him, the room was sealed off, and the young man died of suffocation. Did you get all that? Let me put it more clearly. Gaspàno was not fucking your sister; he only happened to be in the room because he wanted to carry her to safety. Is everything clear to you? Can I stop worrying?"

She did not answer. Puglisi grew concerned, thinking she wasn't really all there.

"Listen to me. If you haven't understood what I just said, and you say something different when asked, my career is over. I'm staging this whole scene only because it didn't seem right to me, and also because you asked me to."

Agatina suddenly jerked her head around and bit his lips till they bled. Taken by surprise, Puglisi instinctively let her go. And this time it was she who grabbed him by the arms and pushed him backwards towards the kitchen.

"Come 'ere! Come 'ere!" she cried.

She was trembling, but only internally, the way cats do sometimes. In the kitchen she lay down on the small table and pulled Puglisi towards her by the lapels of his jacket.

"Please! Please!" she implored him, breathing hard.

"No," said Puglisi, trying to force her hands open. He succeeded, but it only made matters worse, because Agatina, once she let go, locked her arms behind his neck, panting.

"Let me go," said Puglisi, who felt his legs begin to shake, and not only because of the position he was in.

She started kissing his face and neck, her motion like that of a bird when eating: a peck here, then back with the head, another peck there, then back again with the head.

"Please," said Puglisi.

"No," she replied. "No."

~~~

"I'm going to call Catalanotti now and have him take you home," said Puglisi. "And you, meanwhile, straighten your-self out."

Agatina, after what had happened between them—biting and scratching and falling off the table and onto the floor as they kept on fucking—appeared a little calmer.

"All right," she said.

Puglisi went out on the landing and called the man he had posted as guard. Catalanotti arrived in a flash, consumed by curiosity as to what might have happened since his supe-rior, and later the woman, had gone upstairs. As soon as he saw the two corpses, he turned pale. The color of their faces and hands upset him; they looked fake, like puppets.

"Oh, shit!"

Then he looked in the kitchen and saw Agatina leaning on the table, with her head in her folded arms.

"I don't know yet who the young man is," Puglisi explained calmly. "He tried to save the widow but died of smoke inhalation."

"Poor things! Poor things, both of them!" Catalanotti cried out in sympathy for the dead, while not failing, in the meantime, to examine the scene with his eyes, like the good cop that he was. There was something about it that didn't convince him, but he couldn't put his finger on it.

"Yes," said Puglisi. "He was a brave lad, but unlucky. He laid a board down between the mound of salt out back and the house, climbed up, and broke the window to come inside—"

"Stop right there," Catalanotti enjoined him in a soft voice.

"Why?" the constable asked, surprised.

"Because all the window panes are intact, and if they're intact, he couldn't have entered the room unless the woman opened the window from the inside."

Puglisi felt like a child caught telling a lie. If not for what he had just done with Agatina, he would never have let himself be hoisted with his own petard like a novice.

"Yeah, you're right," he said, embarrassed. "So how do you explain it?"

"No doubt about it," said Catalanotti. "Here's how I explain it."

He took four paces, sidestepping the dead man, went up to the French door, opened both sides, and went out onto the balcony under a driving rain, a real deluge. He took a red-and-white-checked handkerchief out of his pocket, wrapped this around his right hand, punched his fist through the pane closest to the handle, making sure that all the shards landed inside, then went back into the room.

"You can continue now, sir," he said sarcastically. "Now your argument makes perfect sense."

Puglisi didn't have time to resume speaking before Catalanotti, already thinking about something else and frowning darkly, went back outside onto the balcony and stared fixedly at a point in the mound of salt.

"What is it?" asked Puglisi, himself going outside into the heavy downpour.

"Over there," said Catalanotti, pointing towards a spot halfway up the mound. "There. I first saw it out of the corner of my eye and didn't pay any attention. Then it came back to me. Look."

Puglisi looked towards the spot the other was indicating to him with his outstretched arm. Sticking out in the middle of the blinding white salt pile was a sort of ball, colored pink and black.

"That wasn't there before," said Puglisi.

"Before when?"

"The first time I looked out this window, it wasn't there. Apparently the rain is bringing it to the surface, so we can see it. What do you think it is?" he asked, but since he already knew the answer, he said, "In my opinion—"

"It's a head, sir. It's the head of a corpse," said Catalanotti. "The head of a pickled corpse."

~~~

While escorting Signora Agatina—who seemed to him strangely calm, given her misfortunes—Catalanotti dropped in at police headquarters to tell his colleague Burruano to hurry and inform the judge of the discovery. Meanwhile, Puglisi, who hadn't expected the additional exertion, began climbing the little mountain of salt in the pouring rain.

He got covered with salt from head to toe, the crystals working their way under his clothing, making Agatina's bites and scratches burn like fire. Several times he slipped back down to the bottom of the mound and had to start his climb all over again, each time with greater difficulty, eyes watering from the salt. In the end he managed to get within reach of the head, and recognized Dr. Gammacurta.

"Doctor! Doctor!" he cried hopelessly.

But a sort of miracle occurred. Gammacurta opened his eyes and looked straight at him, recognizing him.

"Oh, it's you?" he managed to articulate with difficulty, but clearly. "Good morning."

Then he dropped his head to one side, closed his eyes, and died.

Puglisi looked him over carefully. There were no visible signs of injury. Then he started to dig away the salt around the doctor's head and chest, and at last he saw a pink sort of paste made of water, salt, and blood.

In endeavoring to describe

In endeavoring to describe the truly painful events that have occasioned such damage and unrest in the town of Vigàta, an integral part of the province of Montelusa for which I humbly embody the function of prefectorial representative of the state, it behooves me to remind Your Most Illustrious Lordship what my sentiments concerning the problems afflicting Sicily have always been. Of the prefects of this island consulted last August, and especially of the four who met in Palermo, I certainly was not in the majority who declared themselves favorable to the continued use of conventional means to achieve the fruitlessly much-desired and much-sought pacification of the island. This was because, rich with the experience handed down to me by my predecessor in this high office, the enlightened Commendator Saverio Foà, who long presided over the destinies of this province, I had looked on in despair as I encountered a province in every way the same as that described to me, one that had already frustrated the efforts and eroded the reputations of so many able and zealous functionaries sent to govern it. In consequence, Your Excellency, who surely know my thoughts on these matters and who saw fit, in your capacity as minister of the interior, to place so high a function on my shoulders, will not be surprised to learn that I—being well familiar, by direct and indirect experience, with the moral perversity of this population, for whom all sense of justice, honesty, and honor remain a dead letter, and who as a result are rapacious, bloody, and superstitious—am of the opinion, and increasingly so, that I should not rule out recourse to any of the exceptional, restrictive legal mea-sures that the government makes available, in the proper circum-stances, yet never implements with the necessary firmness required.

The events that occurred yesterday evening in Vigàta painfully confirm what I have been thinking for some time, since, all other considerations aside, what happened on the occasion of the new the-atre of Vigàta's opening to the public has the very hallmarks of a genuine popular uprising, incited by a few agitators, against my per-son as representative of the state. While others may think differently and support their positions with nothing more than empty rumors, it is clear that this was a seditious rebellion aimed at overthrowing and defeating the authority of the state in this Sicilian province. I present this pure and simple fact, that it may prove valid by the power of its truth.

When I assumed my high office, the theatre of Vigàta had already been almost entirely built, lacking only a few embellishments of little importance. As it was my responsibility to appoint the mem-bers of the Adminstrative Council, I proposed to nominate two prom-inent figures from Vigàta and four from Montelusa, as the proximity of the provincial capital seemed certain to contribute to the prosperity of the theatre itself to a greater degree than the people of Vigàta could ever do, being scarcely interested in matters of art. When apprised of the composition of the council, the two Vigatese members immediately resigned, citing miserably parochial reasons for their action. In order to avoid harmful delays and useless polemics, I replaced the two appointed members from Vigàta with two exemplary citizens of Montelusa. The president of the Administrative Council, the Marchese Antonino Pio di Condò, a man of lofty sentiment and exquisite sensibility, one day happened to ask me cordially if I had any suggestions as to the opera that should be performed for the inaugural soirée, an event that must certainly be solemn in character. Entirely by chance, a title came to mind, that of The Brewer of Preston, *an opera I had occasion to enjoy in my greener years—to wit, at its triumphal première in Florence in 1847.*

I cited this work not for personal reasons, of course, but because I considered the opera, in its fanciful lightness, its simplicity of word and music, appropriate for the Sicilians'—and more specifically, the Vigatese's—undeveloped appreciation of the more sublime manifestations of art. It was, I say, a simple, cordial suggestion on my part, but the marchese, a good patriot and noted exponent of the governing party, happened to interpret it, mistakenly, as an order—an order which I, in truth, had neither the power nor the intention to give. Upon learning that the suggestion came from me, a few members of the Administrative Council, Freemasons and Mazzinians in league with Freemasons and Mazzinians in Vigàta, fiercely and prejudicially opposed it, spreading in bad faith the rumor that the idea was not a simple suggestion on my part but a precise order. The Marchese Antonino Pio di Condò, offended by vile accusations that he was a man always ready to bow down to authority, irrevocably resigned. Commendator Massimo Però, a man of sound judgment and good sense, was then elected to replace him. It was at this time that Professor Artidoro Ragona, a member of the council, took it upon himself to recommend the same opera, having meanwhile had the opportunity to appreciate it during a recent sojourn in Naples. This occurred, I am keen to point out, without any intervention whatsoever on my part. And yet, this fact, too, became the subject of malicious gossip, according to which the relationship between Commendator Però's recommendation and the victory of his son, Dr. Achille Però, in the recent competition for the office of first secretary of the prefecture of Montelusa was hardly coincidental. I must likewise at this point declare firmly that neither was the well-deserved success of the worthy young Achille Però in any way owing to the good offices of one Mr.

Emanuele Ferraguto, as some have spitefully insinuated. Mr. Ferraguto, a man of lofty sentiment, of highly civic disposition and generous mind, is . . .

~~~

To His Excillince the Perfict Bortuzzi
Montelusa

Dear Perfict,

Your a grate big sonofabich. Why don you go becka to Florince? Your not a perfict but a big fat stinkin turd enn a jeckass. Tree peple died coz a you inna fire inna teater. Your the biggest crook of all. You got no conshinz.

a citizin

~~~

To His Ixcillincy Bortuzzi Prephict of Montelusa

Stop breaking the balls of the Vigatese. The opra you want isna gonna play. Fuhgettabouttit, iss better fuh you.

The People of Vigàta.

~~~

My children, dear parishioners in the Lord,

Like the wound of Jesus nailed to the Cross, the wound in my side is losing more bile than blood these days, believe me. An atheistic, blasphemous municipal council has had a theatre built in this upstanding, industrious town and will open it tomorrow with the performance of an opera. Do not go to see it, beloved sons and daughters! For the very instant you set foot inside that building, your souls shall be lost for all eternity! But perhaps you don't believe what your old parish priest is telling you; surely you think I am joking or have turned senile. And perhaps it's true that my mind is not what it used to be; but, then, I am not speaking now in my own words, but in the words of people whose minds are far greater than mine and all of yours put together. Thus I say to you, and I repeat: the theatre is the devil's house of preference! Saint Augustine—who nevertheless was someone who had led a bad, wicked life, who went to brothels and coupled with foul, plague-ridden women and used to get drunk as a monkey—Saint Augustine, I say, tells us that once upon a time in Carthage, which is a city near here, over in Africa, he entered a theatre and saw a performance of naked men and women doing lewd things, and when he went home afterwards, he couldn't fall asleep all night, so afflicted was he by what he had seen!

And I would also like to tell you another story, a story told by Tertullian, who is hardly chickenshit but a very great mind. Tertullian tells that once, a devout woman, a respected mother of a family, got it in her head that she had to go to the theatre at all costs. Neither her husband, nor brother, nor mother, nor children could talk her out of it. And so the stubborn woman saw the performance, but when she came out, she was not the same. She cursed, she mouthed obscenities, she wanted every man she passed to mount her right there on the street. Thus her husband and sons brought her back home by force and quickly called a priest. The priest sprinkled the woman with holy water and commanded the devil to come out. And do you know what the devil said?

He said: "You, priest, get your hands off my things! I took this woman for myself, because she went into my house, which is the theatre, of her own accord!"

And when the woman died, her soul was damned, because the holy priest could do nothing for her. Do you, my dear parishioners, want to be taken by the devil? Do you want to damn your souls? The theatre is the house of the devil! It is the place of the devil! And that place deserves the same fire that God unleashed upon Sodom and Gomorrah! Fire! Fire!

~~~

Right Reverend Canon
G. Verga—Mother Church—Vigàta

Yesterday I went to church and heard your sermon against the theatre. And a question came to mind: the woman you have kept at the rectory and in your bed for twenty years and with whom you even had a son by the name of Giugiuzzo, aged fifteen, what category of whore does she belong to? Is she a woman of the theatre, a woman of Sodom, a woman of Gomorrah, or a simple slut?

Sincerely,

A parishioner who believes in God's things

~~~

. . . and as concerns the company of mounted militiamen employed by H. E. the Prefect Bortuzzi to implement illegal measures of repression, my opinion cannot help but concur with that of the majority of the Sicilian people, who consider this military unit to have been from the start in league with the Mafia and the organized criminal groups of the countryside. Given the already delicate situation, the intervention of the mounted soldiers further stoked the passions of the Vigatese, who regarded it as an additional abuse of power, especially as neither the army, as clearly ordered by yourself, my lord Lieutenant General Casanova, nor the regular police Forces of Public Safety, represented in this town by police lieutenant Puglisi, a man unanimously deemed of unimpeachable conduct, much less the Royal Corps of Carabinieri, who for three days had been confined to barracks as a

precautionary measure by Major Santhià, their commander, took part in the police operation deemed indispensable by the prefect.

It is not my place to express any judgment whatsoever concerning the methods of His Excellency Bortuzzi either before or after the distressing events that occurred that night in Vigàta.

I cannot, however, refrain from calling to your attention that during the entire time in question there was a certain person in the company of the prefect, one Emanuele Ferraguto, whom the carabinieri have several times recommended should be considered for legal internment, only to be prevented from proceeding by the express will of the prefect himself and the local magistrature.

I also call to your attention, although the question does not fall within the jurisdiction invested in me, that this same Emanuele Ferraguto was granted permission to bear arms by the direct intercession of the prefect with the commissioner of police.

Respectfully yours,

Colonel Armando Vidusso
Royal Army Commander for Montelusa

⌁

To H. E. Vincenzo Spanò, Esq.
President of the Court of Montelusa

Were you aware that the impresario of the opera The Brewer of Preston, *which will be performed the day after tomorrow at Vigàta, is Signor Pilade Spadolini, son of a sister of the prefect Bortuzzi's brother-in-law? Just so you know, so that the proper measures may be taken.*

A group of loyal citizens of Vigàta

⌁

To His Excellency the Prefect Umberto Bortuzzi
Prefecture of Montelusa
Personal and confidential

When I came to Vigàta this morning for reconnaissance concerning the disposition of the forces of order tomorrow evening, I had occasion to notice that a number of walls of the buildings giving onto the Corso had been defaced with the following words, written repeatedly:

THE PREFUCKT DON'T KNOW WHEN TO QUIT
LET'S MAKE HIM SINK IN HIS OWN SHIT

I deduced from the curious noun in the first line that the offensive words were directed at Your Most Excellent person.

I have thus given orders that these shameful writings be covered with whitewash.

I remain Your Excellency's most devoted

Villaroel

∿∿∿

To the Commissioner of Police
Dr. Cavaliere Everardo—Montelusa

Your Excellency,

This morning I received a message from you in which you asked me for a precise and detailed report concerning the events that occurred last night in Vigàta. In order to conduct a serious and thorough investigation, I shall need at least one week. As you yourself probably know, the number of confirmed deaths is three (two as a result of the fire, one by firearms). The wounded number twenty-five between burn victims and those suffering contusions from the riot in the theatre. In my humble opinion, however, what is presently at issue is not so much the investigation itself as the manner in which it should be presented to the public. I shall need, therefore, prior instructions from you on how to proceed, since the matter seems rather complicated to me and of such a nature as to risk being prejudicial to the high authorities of the state.

Ever faithfully at your service,

Lieutenant Detective Puglisi

~~~

To Lutenant Puglisi
Comander of the riffraff coppers of Vigàta

Your a shit of a man who takes advantage of women

~~~

To Totò Pennica—Vigàta
the fisherman who lives by the school

Totò, your sister-in-law was a slut who burned to death on top of a man who also burned up in her house. Your wife, who now and then you give a good hiding to, and for good reason, is a slut just like her sister. A case in point: the morning she went to her sister's place and found her burnt up with a man in her room, why didn't she scream and faint like all the women in the world instead of staying up there in that room all quiet for an hour with the police lieutenant?

Oh, what a beautiful day!

"Oh, what a beautiful day! What a fine spring sky!" Everardo Colombo, police commissioner of Montelusa, said aloud as he opened the bedroom curtains.

For most of the nine months since he had moved to the island, it had been raining, sometimes pouring as in the time of Noah's ark, sometimes sprinkling as though shaken from an aspergillum. And this had annoyed him no small amount, even though rain, in Milan, was like one of the family. That, indeed, was the problem: in Montelusa water from the sky seemed utterly foreign. The houses, the landscapes, the people, even the animals, all seemed like they were made to bask in sunlight.

He glanced over at the bed where Signora Pina was still asleep, savoring with a lustful eye the hills and valleys his wife's body formed under the blanket. He decided to give it a try. If by some miracle the attempt succeeded, he did have half an hour at his disposal before going downstairs, where his office was. He sat down beside the bed, on a level with his wife's face, and caressed her cheek ever so lightly, as if his finger were a feather or a breath of wind.

"Pina! My bright little star!"

The wife, who had been eyeing him through half-closed lids for the past fifteen minutes, pretended to wake up with studied slowness. She opened one eye, stared at her husband a moment, curled her lips in a pout that would have made a dead man hard, and turned away without saying a word. Because of that movement, and the rising and falling of the blanket, the commissioner got a whiff of female effluvia strong enough to make him start sweating.

"Get up, my little piglet!" said Everardo, with the appropriate bedroom voice.

"*Lendenatt!*" she said in Milanese.[1]

The commissioner was not deterred by the insult.

"Come, darling, move your *coo*![2] Didn't you hear the grandfather clock? It's chiming nine and you're still in bed!"

"*Cagon!*"[3]

Again the commissioner took it in stride and bent over, letting his lips graze her ear. This time his wife turned her head slightly towards him.

"*Coppet*, you stupid man!"[4]

Despite the lady's manifest opposition, Everardo decided to give it one last try. He began caressing his wife's ample buttocks, which offered themselves to him in all their glory, his hand moving first very gently, then ever more clingingly, slow as a snail.

"Oh, my soul!"

"That's my bottom, not your soul," Signora Pina said frostily, casting the hand off her crupper with a thrust of the hips.

"That's what I deserve! That's what I get for marrying a washerwoman's daughter!" said the commissioner, indignant, standing up. And for good measure, he added:

---

1 Idiot.
2 Bottom, bum.
3 Asshole.
4 Fuck off; get stuffed.

"I'm going to go pee!"

He went out of the bedroom, slamming the door behind him. In the privy, finding himself cramped, his rage increased in inverse proportion to the amount of space around him. He began punching the wall. The problem with his wife had been going on for some ten days now, ever since he had told her they would not be attending the inauguration of the new theatre of Vigàta.

"And why not?" she had asked.

"What the hell do you care? I have my reasons."

"What? I had a dress made for the occasion! Did you hear me, you wretch?"

"We have to be sensible, Pina. I don't much like all these problems the prefect has with the people of Vigàta. Enough of his persecution and intrigues! Bortuzzi is a madman! With him, the way things are going, we'll end up between the shit house and the sewer. Forget about the whole thing."

"Oh, yes?"

"Yes. And that's enough."

The commissioner's wife, who had been polishing her nails, then stood up very slowly. With her right forefinger, she had pointed to the part of her body where Everardo Colombo, twice a week, found gold, incense, and myrrh.

"This is mine," Donna Pina had said, standing tall and stern and terrible as an oracle. "And I'm never going to give it to you again. From now on you can let your balls flap in the wind, as far as I'm concerned."

And she had kept her word.

⌐⌐⌐

The commissioner's anger began to subside as he descended the great staircase that led from the fourth floor of the Royal

Police Commissariat to the third. True, further headaches awaited him there, but so did the tangible symbols of his power, of what he had managed to achieve in the space of only a few years.

"Good morning, Cavaliere," police officer Alfonso Sala-mone greeted him. Salamone had been assigned to guard the commissioner's private apartment for two reasons: first, because his legs had been shattered by several shots from the carbine of a fugitive, and second, because Signora Pina, some six months earlier, had stubbornly insisted that she wanted him and only him. The lady claimed, in fact—though it was anybody's guess why—that with Salamone she could feel certain that no malefactor would ever succeed in penetrating her living quarters.

"But who do you think would ever come up here?" her husband had asked at the time. "A thief at the commissariat? Imagine that!"

But she would not be dissuaded. She wanted Salamone, and she got Salamone.

"How are the legs today, Salamone?"

And how are your horns? the guard wanted to say, but restrained himself.

"Better today, sir," he said instead.

At the landing, the commissioner turned right, where the antechamber, the secretariat, and his enormous office were. Some five or six people, who had been waiting since dawn to talk to him, rose and bowed the moment he entered.

"Good morning, Your Excellency," they said in chorus.

Colombo raised a hand, showing three spread fingers—either in greeting or paternalistic benediction, it wasn't clear which—then went into the secretariat, where there wasn't a living soul, and threw open the half-closed door of his office.

He was engulfed by a burst of light, the curtains of the great window having already been opened, allowing the sun to pour in.

"What a splendid morning!"

"If it doesn't turn, Cavaliere."

The tone of voice and phrasing of his first secretary, Dr. Francesco Meli—who always dressed in black and always wore an expression as if his entire family had been wiped out the day before by an earthquake—stopped him from continuing his paean to the day. Was the secretary, standing beside the desk looking like an effigy of the Day of the Dead, referring only to the weather, or was he alluding to a bit of bad news?

"What's wrong?" the commissioner asked, changing expression.

"In Fela a man nobody recognized entered the local social club and shot and killed Nunzio Peritore, a land surveyor by profession with a clean record, who was playing *tresette* and *briscola* with three other people."

"Are you telling me the others didn't recognize the man who stood there and killed him?"

The first secretary heaved a long sigh before answering. He looked afflicted by an even greater suffering than usual.

"Cavaliere, one of them was under the table because one of his shoelaces was untied; the second, also under the table, was picking up a card that had fallen on the floor; and the third, at that precise moment, got a *muschitta* in his ear."

"A what?"

"A mosquito, sir."

"All Sicilians, these cardplayers?"

"No, Cavaliere. The man tying his shoe was Giulio Vendramin, a Venetian. He's a traveling salesman."

"Anything else?"

Meli let out another anguished sigh.

"Lieutenant Puglisi of Vigàta has brought to our attention the presence of a dangerous Roman republican by the name of Nando Traquandi. The Ministry of Justice has a warrant out for his arrest."

"That son of a whore Mazzini has been spotted in Naples. Apparently he wants to come here to the island and meanwhile is sending scouts ahead to get a feel for the place. Has Puglisi found out who's sheltering Traquandi?"

"Yessir. He's staying at the home of Don Giuseppe Mazzaglia, who's someone that certainly doesn't hide what he thinks."

"Tell Puglisi to arrest them at once, Traquandi and Mazzaglia. Let's get them out of our hair."

Meli seemed to plunge into an abyss of despair.

"What's wrong, Meli?"

"Well, you see, Cavaliere, Don Pippino Mazzaglia is not just anybody. He's loved by everyone in Vigàta. He's a man who's always ready to give everything he has to help others. If we go after him, all of Vigàta will turn against us. And there's an ill wind blowing these days in Vigàta, thanks to Prefect Bortuzzi. Do we want to add fuel to the fire? We could start by arresting only Traquandi."

"Seems we're in quite a pickle," the commissioner said pensively.

He got up, put his hands in his pockets, went up to the window, and basked in the sunlight.

"Let's do this," he said, turning around. "Tell Puglisi to arrest Traquandi the day after the opera performance in Vigàta. The day after, is that clear?"

"Perfectly," said Meli. "But, if I may, sir, why the day

after? That might be too late. By then the man may have gone to another town and we will have lost track of him."

"Too late, blockhead? The Vigatese are like rats. Give them a second chance, and they'll make even more mayhem. So, repeat: What did I just say?"

"To arrest Traquandi the day after the opera performance in Vigàta. But not to touch Don Pippino Mazzaglia."

"Very good. Is there anything else?"

"Yes, Cavaliere. Forgive me for insisting, but why arrest Traquandi three days from now?"

"You haven't understood a blasted thing," the commissioner cut him off.

~~~

At about ten o'clock that same morning, Tano Barreca, a young representative of La Parisienne, a Palermo perfume and cosmetics house, appeared before Salamone the guard.

He came once every fortnight, and had been doing so for the past six months.

"Can I go up? Is the lady at home alone?"

"Go ahead, she's at home."

"And don't forget: at any sign of danger, whistle."

"Oh, I'll whistle, don't you worry about that."

The prearranged whistle from Salamone, for which Signora Pina paid him handsomely, would spare both the commissioner's wife and young Barreca an embarrassing scene, to say the least.

Their biweekly encounter always unfolded in the same manner. Without knocking on the door, Barreca would enter Signora Pina's bedroom, where she lay ready for him in bed, naked, legs spread. Barreca would carelessly drop on her dressing table the perfumes and creams he had brought with

him, take off his shoes, socks, jacket, shirt, jersey, and under-
wear, and, in a single bound, plunge into the tight, firm flesh
of the commissioner's wife. They would go the first round,
which lasted two minutes, in silence, and in his mind Barreca
would devote those minutes to his father, Santo Barreca,
arrested some twenty times by people like the husband of
Signora Pina, whom he was fucking at that moment. Then he
would lie down beside her, breathing heavily and holding his
hand over her crack, all the while letting that hand fidget
about without respite, and he would count to two hundred,
settle back in between the lady's thighs, and go the second
round, which lasted three minutes, this time devoting his
exploit to his brother Sarino Barreca, who was killed while
trying to escape from La Vicaria prison by people like the
husband of Signora Pina, whom he was fucking at that
moment. Then he would lie down beside her, breathing heavily and holding his hand over her crack, all the while letting
that hand fidget without respite, and he would count to three
hundred, then settle back in between the lady's thighs, devoting the third coupling to himself, since one day or another he
would surely end up being sent to prison by people like the
husband of Signora Pina, whom he was fucking at that
moment. And the third round was long, unrelenting, and
breathless. Then came the moment when Tano would begin
to ask respectfully:

"Is Signora coming? Are you coming, Signora?"

Yet the signora had never deigned to reply.

That morning, however, overwrought as she was from
conjugal abstinence, when the young man breathlessly
repeated the question in tempo with his in-and-out motion,
the unhappy woman answered:

"Yes . . . Yes . . . I'm coming! . . . co-o-ming . . . Oooohhh!"

◆◆◆

At twelve noon on the dot, Cavaliere Colombo signed his last document, set down his pen, raised his arms, stretched, and let out a long sigh. His morning's work was finally over. He and Meli exchanged glances.

"Well, I'm going to go," said the secretary. "Any orders, Cavaliere?"

"See you at three, my dear Meli," said the commissioner, dismissing him.

And he watched the secretary walk away. Meli was slightly lame. Colombo had even been tempted to sack him less than a week after taking office, but then he had realized how very useful the man could be. Once, for example, after he had given him an order in Milanese, Meli had got it all backwards, and as a result did the exact opposite of what he'd been told. At the time, Colombo had flown into a rage, but then he realized that his secretary could become a perfect alibi for him: he could always blame him for not having understood what he had been told.

The commissioner stood up, walked through the empty secretariat and anteroom, and found himself face-to-face with Salamone, the guard.

"How goes it?"

"Fine, Excellency. And yourself?"

"Fine, fine."

And it's a good thing, thought Salamone, *that your horns don't yet reach the chandelier.*

◆◆◆

At table, the commissioner noticed that his spouse's eyes were sparkling and her complexion rosy. She seemed to be in a good mood. So, to show her just who he was, he started tell-ing her about Traquandi the Mazzinian. He had not had him immediately arrested, he explained, because he, as commis-sioner, might be able to profit from it. Indeed, if the opera the prefect was imposing on the people of Vigàta were to go badly, he could gain a two-point advantage over that other representative of the state by then arresting the dangerous agitator. If, instead, the opera went well, he could still even the score by making a big show of sending the subversive rat to prison. Traquandi, in short, was an ace up his sleeve, to be played at the most opportune moment.

"What do you think, Pina?"

The answer was violent and brutal.

"I don't think. I only know that when I look at you, I feel like throwing up. Go get stuffed!"

How much longer is this going to last?

"How much longer is this going to last? Let's have a look at the watch," said Commendator Restuccia. Seeing the hour, he made a rough guess that the second act would be over soon. He turned to his wife, who had fallen into a deep sleep, and shook her arm. She gave a start and opened her eyes.

"What is it?" she asked, alarmed.

"Nothing, Assunta. As soon as they finish singing and Act Two is over, we're going to stand up, get our coats, and go home."

At that very moment, from the gallery, came the angry voice of Lollò Sciacchitano.

"Nobody is going to make a monkey out of me, understand? Nobody in heaven or on earth! The man who makes a fool of me has yet to be born! Look at them! Four shits singing and thinking they can put one over on me!"

Lollò had it in for the people singing onstage, who looked out at him in turn, goggle-eyed.

In a flash Lieutenant Puglisi rose from the orchestra where he had been sitting, went out into the corridor, and climbed the steps to the gallery to find out for himself what the hell was going through Lollò's head. Instead he literally ran straight into one of Villaroel's militiamen, who promptly seized him and pinned him up against the wall.

"Let go of me at once or I'll break your skull," said Puglisi, trembling with rage. "I'm the superintendent of police."

"Excuse me, sir, I didn't recognize you," said the other, immediately taking his hands off him.

Puglisi meanwhile noticed that another ten or so armed soldiers were standing guard in the corridor that surrounded the orchestra.

"What are you doing here?"

"Prefect's orders, sir. Nobody is to leave the theatre."

Jesus Christ, this fucking prefect is going to trigger another '48! Puglisi said to himself, and began taking the stairs to the gallery two at a time. When he arrived, it, too, was surrounded by militiamen, just like the corridors behind the boxes. He dashed straight for Lollò Sciacchitano, who was still squirming and hollering as a number of friends were trying to calm him down.

"What's going on, Lollò?" asked Puglisi, who knew exactly how to handle the raving lunatic. "Has someone done you wrong?" Seeing the policeman, Lollò seemed to grow a little calmer. The two liked each other, even if they never talked about it.

"They certainly have! They want to take me for a fool!"

"Who wants to take you for a fool?"

"These theatre people. The program says there are two twin brothers, one named George and the other Daniel! It ain't true, Lieutenant, or I'm a blind man! It's always the same person changing his clothes and pretending to be first the one guy and then the other! But I got good eyes, I do!"

"Excuse me, Lollò, but what the hell do you care?"

"What do you mean, what do I care? I paid for a ticket to see two twins! An' what I got is one guy pretending he's two! You don't believe me? Just try calling both of them out onstage, and you'll see, only one o' them'll appear."

Puglisi was struggling to think of a response that would be equal to Lollò's ironclad logic when, with a final *zoom zoom* from the orchestra, the second act drew to a close.

∿∿∿

As the curtain was still falling, people were already getting up, some to return home, others to go smoke a cigar, the ladies to go chat, when onstage appeared Captain Villaroel, looking like a puppet, in full dress uniform with plumed cap, gloves, and parade sabre. He raised a hand to stop the movement of people.

"Your polite attention, please," he began.

His sudden appearance paralyzed everyone, freezing them in whatever gesture they were making at that moment.

"By order of His Excellency the Prefect Bortuzzi, to avoid any public disorder, everyone still here is commanded to remain here. What I mean is, you can't even go out into the corridors. You are all ordered to remain in your seats."

This time Puglisi got scared in earnest. A strange noise began to rise from the orchestra, the boxes, and the gallery. It was as if a great big pot, covered by an equally gigantic lid, had reached the boiling point. The policeman realized it was the menacing murmurs of the people in the audience.

Villaroel again raised his hand.

"His Excellency the Prefect invites all the citizens of Vigàta to listen to this . . ." The captain paused. To his horror he realized he couldn't think of the word.

"Bullshit?" a voice from the gallery suggested with fraternal solicitude.

"Caca?" another seconded him from the orchestra.

But then Villaroel's memory came back to him, and he was able to start over from the beginning in a firmer tone.

"His Excellency the Prefect invites all the citizens of Vigàta to listen to this opera attentively, without doing or saying anything that might offend this high authority of the state, who is here in person."

And he turned his back and left. At that very moment, Puglisi hopped like a cricket over two rows of seats and dashed towards Mommo Friscia, who, as the policeman had noticed a second earlier, was filling his lungs with air as his face turned as round as a melon. He succeeded in putting his hand over the man's mouth before he was able to do what he intended to do.

Mommo Friscia's raspberries were legendary in town and beyond. They had the power, density, and brutality of a devastating earthquake or other natural disaster. The Honorable Nitto Sammartano, member of parliament, had seen a brilliant political career, one that would certainly have carried him to a ministerial post, go up in smoke because of an unexpected raspberry unleashed by Friscia in the middle of a crowded assembly. Not that Mommo was opposed to the politican, mind you; he had done it just to do it, in a moment of artistic inspiration. The loftier, more vibrant and stentorian the words, the more irresistible his urge to let fly. And Sammartano never recovered from that historic raspberry during the assembly. A sort of shock ran through his body every time he was about to open his mouth in public; his thoughts would cloud up and he would start stammering.

Now, at that moment, with all the commotion there was in the theatre, a raspberry from Friscia would have been like a trumpet sounding the call to revolution. Puglisi held his hand over Mommo's mouth until he saw him turning purple for lack of breath, then he let go, since the palm of his hand was burning as if it had snuffed out a bomb fuse. Meanwhile he started to hear a powerful chorus of voices, consisting not only of those of the singers but of the audience as well.

"Cold! Cold! Getting warmer! Hot!"

Bewildered, he looked towards the stage. Villaroel was having trouble finding the opening between the curtains that would lead him out.

He shuffled first to the right ("Cold! Cold!") then to the left ("Cold! Cold!"), and only when he was right in the middle did the audience shout "Hot! Hot!" Yet when he tried to separate the heavy velvet fabric with his hands, he encountered only abundant folds, never any opening. At last a stagehand came to his aid and held the two ends of the curtain open for him. As Villaroel made his exit, the audience erupted in warm applause, the first and last of the evening, combined with shouts of "Bravo!" and "Well done!" The mayor of Vigàta, who felt more horrified by his fellow townsfolk's irony than he would have been by a shootout, stood up, pale as a corpse.

"Friends, townsmen," he began in a quavering voice. "I beg you, please, for God's sake—"

He wasn't able to finish. Before the eyes of everyone, the prefect grabbed him by the sleeve and forced him to sit back down.

"What the hell's got into you? You're begging whom? These people should be shot! Just sit tight and don't make any trouble!"

~~~

Behind the curtain, the stage crew was changing the décor at high speed. Despite the thickness of the velvet, the people in the audience could hear loud shouts, curses, racing footsteps, and hammering upon hammering. Then, after everything in the auditorium seemed to have calmed down, once again the very loud voice of Lollò Sciacchitano rang out.

"I need to pee! I need to go pee and those fucking bastard soldiers won't let me! I think I'm gonna pee down on the orchestra!"

Suddenly, as if on command, the entire audience, men as well as women, needed to relieve themselves. Two or three ladies started squirming in their seats, hands on their bellies.

Commendator Restuccia, seeing his wife in desperate straits, grabbed the walking stick he never parted with, and ordered his wife:

"Come with me!"

Once in the corridor, a militiaman blocked his way.

"Where are you going?"

"I am taking my wife to go pee. Got anything against that?"

"Yes. The prefect forbids it."

"Let's talk about this," the commendatore said calmly, pulling on the handle of his walking stick with his right hand; out came a blade nearly a foot and half long. What he had was not a walking stick, but a very sharp swordstick.

"Go right ahead," said the soldier, stepping aside.

Meanwhile the mayor, at the prefect's suggestion, had stood up again and was gesticulating for the audience to listen.

"Fellow citizens!" he said. "Everyone who needs to go to the privy can tell the soldiers, who will escort them there."

Half the audience rose and left the theatre, and quarrels began to break out in front of the rest rooms over who had priority.

At last the third act began. The stage featured the gallery of a castle, with the throne room in the background, glimpsed through a broad doorway. The singers all sang that they were awaiting the arrival of the king.

"What king?" asked Signora Restuccia, who, after relieving herself, felt more interested in matters of art and life.

"What the hell are you asking? What king? How should I know? Who understands anything about this opera anyway?" the commendatore exploded, and he added: "Go back to sleep; it's better that way."

"Honor! Honor! Honor!
To the valiant victor!
By him are England's shores
Delivered from all wars."

Singing onstage were the same people who had sung before as brewers, then as soldiers, now all dressed up in aristocratic finery, though their faces remained the same. Puglisi cast a worried glance up at the gallery where Lollò Sciacchitano was sitting, but Lollò was squabbling with someone seated near him and didn't notice what was happening onstage.

For no apparent reason, the entire audience had become calm and serene. Perhaps people had grown tired of talking and laughing and were patiently waiting for the whole thing finally to end. The prefect looked slightly less enraged.

Villaroel was back at Bortuzzi's side, sitting with his upper body hunched forward, since his plume was so high that it touched the ceiling of the royal box. Don Memè, a smile cutting his face in two from ear to ear and making him look just like a pomegranate, was on the other side of the prefect. But between him and His Excellency sat Donna Giagia, the prefect's wife, who kept so still she looked like a statue. The last guest in the royal box, the mayor, was holding his head in his hands, lips moving silently. He was praying.

Puglisi left the orchestra—no longer stopped by the soldiers, who now recognized him—went halfway down the corridor, opened a door, and found himself on a landing with stairs leading up to the stage and down to the understage. He took the first staircase and ended up in the wings, just a step away from the people singing. He saw a man in coat and tails, nervous and sweaty, wiping his forehead with a once-white handkerchief.

"Good evening," he said. "I'm Lieutenant Puglisi, police. Will this be over anytime soon?"

"Let's say half an hour. But I'm very worried."

"Me, too," said Puglisi.

"I'm worried for Maddalena, the soprano singing the part of Effy. She's very upset, you know. Because of what's happening in the audience. During the intermission she fainted on me, and I had to give her smelling salts. Afterwards she didn't want to go back out onstage. I don't know if she can hold up till the end."

"That's all we need. But, if you don't mind my asking, who are you?"

"I'm the impresario. The name's Pilade Spadolini. I'm His Excellency the Prefect's nephew."

All in the family, Puglisi thought, but said nothing.

"Okay, watch; here comes the most delicate moment, the duet between Effy and Anne. This is where Maddalena has to give it her all."

"And so, what do you say?" Effy sang from the stage with a mocking expression, addressing the other woman, Anne. Then, turning her back to her and looking at the audience: *"(I want to have a little fun)."*

But, to judge from her facial expression and her trembling hands, it was clear she wasn't having any fun at all.

"I say I'll be his bride!" Anne answered firmly, staring at her with a fiery eye and putting her hands on her hips.

"Maybe yes, maybe no. Ha ha ha!"

"You laugh?" asked Anne, half bewildered, half angry.

"Yes, I laugh because you're not yet convinced," said Effy, who seemed more and more determined to make her rival quit the stage mad with rage.

"No! No!" the other said desperately.

"I'll give you some advice, for your own . . ."

The word Effy had yet to say was *"good"*—that is, *"for your own good"*—but since the music allowed it, between *"your own"* and *"good,"* she stopped, filled her lungs with air to belt out the high note, and opened her mouth.

At that exact moment the militiaman Tinuzzo Bonavia, who suffered from attacks of narcolepsy as abrupt as they were unstoppable, suddenly fell asleep on his feet right where he was standing guard—in other words, right in front of the half-open door that led directly to the stage and the understage. As soon as he nodded off, his hands, which had been holding his carbine, went limp; the rifle slipped, fell to the floor butt-first, and fired. The sudden blast of the shot, amplified by the theatre's acoustics, made everyone jump up in the air—singers, musicians, and audience—while the bullet grazed Bonavia's nose, which started him bleeding like a pig with its throat slit and squealing like the same animal an instant before the slaughter. Thus Effy, who by now had enough air in her lungs to propel a sailing ship, let loose her *"good"* a fraction of a second after the shot rang out—but, because of her sudden fright, what came out of her throat, instead of *"good,"* was a kind of raucus, powerful steamboat siren so potent that to some of the people in attendance who had navigated the Northern seas, it actually sounded like the terrifying whistle a whale emits when harpooned. Commendator Restuccia's wife jolted out of a deep sleep and, not knowing what was happening, added the last straw. She screamed. Now, the screams of Signora Restuccia were no laughing matter. When informed, for example, of her mother's death, the commendatore's wife screamed once, and only once, but it was enough to shatter the glass of the neighboring houses.

The combination of the rifle shot, the cries of the injured militiaman, the soprano's terrifying *"good,"* and Signora Restuccia's shriek triggered uncontrolled panic, aggravated by the fact that nobody was watching the stage. Had they been, they would have had a better sense of the situation; instead, everything happening at once caught them by surprise. After they all rose in fright from their seats, all it took was for the first person to start running before everyone else did the same. Screaming, cursing, yelling, crying, imploring, and praying, some dashed madly out of the auditorium only to run straight into the militiamen blocking their path.

Meanwhile the soprano, after hitting the wrong note, fell to the boards with a thud, out cold.

I am an elementary school teacher

"Iam an elementary school teacher, and I have a family," said Minicuzzo Adornato, the carpenter's son. And he added, to be precise: "A wife and two children."

Commendator Restuccia lit his cigar very slowly, as if on purpose.

"And is this why you didn't say a word against your father's arrest, knowing he was as innocent as Christ?" he asked after taking a first puff.

"Yessir, that's why," the teacher replied, turning red with repressed anger. "I have no power, Commendatore, I'm a nobody, a doormat. And the fact that I have a family means that the minute I make a move, the minute I create a stir or raise a protest or holler, the state will make me pay for it, by the handful and by the bushel; they'll give me the works, pull out all the stops, do whatever they want. And the next day I'll find myself teaching how to write the word *Italy* in some god-forsaken village in Sardinia. Do you get the picture?"

"The state?" Restuccia said calmly looking him in the eye.

"The state, the state. Or do you think the prefect represents the Society for Agricultural Development? Or the Consortium for Land Reclamation? Or the Bel Canto

Association? He *is* the state, Commendatore, with all its laws, carabinieri, judges, and power. And all these forces will come together to stick it to me. And even if they realize that Bortuzzi is a son of a much-fucked whore, they will never tell him he's wrong, because he's one of them, one of those who make up the state."

"You're right, but allow me to ask you a question. Is your father part of your family?"

"Of course."

"So why don't you defend him, the way you would defend, say, your children or your wife?"

Caught unawares by the question, Minicuzzo Adornato didn't answer. So the commendatore, feeling no pity for him, continued.

"A family is a family, my dear friend. And it must always be defended. That's why I'm here. I came to see you to lend you a hand."

"Why?"

"First, because of my grandson Mariolo. And second, because I don't think that someone who thinks that the state is shit—pardon my language—should convince himself that he has to be up to his neck in it."

"Forget about the state," said the schoolteacher. "What's your grandson Mariolo got to do with this?"

"Do you remember when I came to see you, five years ago, to thank you for what you had done for my grandson?"

"I was only doing my duty. He was a spirited boy, and I—"

"He was twisted and you straightened him out. He'd lost his father and mother in a terrible accident and we, his grandparents, didn't know how to help him. There were times when I felt like sticking his head in the tub and letting him drown, the way you do with puppies you don't want to raise."

"What are you saying?!"

"The truth, dear friend, the bitter, naked truth."

"Stop talking rubbish! Your grandson Mariolo is a very fine young man!"

"Of course he is. But it was you who made him that way, first by giving him a few thrashings, and then by making him see reason, through patience, sweat, and effort. And he wasn't your son or grandson."

"It's my job."

"As far as jobs are concerned, you'll forgive me if I say I know a lot more than you do. I'm the head of a company that provides manpower at the port. There is no labor there that isn't done by my men: loading sulfur, almonds, fava beans, or unloading merchandise and machinery. So when it comes to knowing who does his job well and who does his job badly, I know a lot more than you."

The schoolteacher extracted a watch from the pocket of his waistcoat and glanced at it.

"I appreciate your support," he said, "but it's getting late and I have to return to the classroom."

"Excuse me just one more minute. I'm here because I was told that the other day, when your father was arrested, you started crying in front of the whole class."

"It's true. And I immediately apologized to my pupils, who were fairly shocked by it. I should have controlled myself better."

"No, in fact you were right to cry. You showed them that your father is part of your family. And that's why I'm here. You see, your father, Don Ciccio, is a truly admirable man who found himself up against a piece of shit—begging the pardon of anyone who can hear me—like the prefect Bortuzzi, only because he publicly said what he thought about the worthless *Brewer of Preston*. And so I took it upon myself to do something about it. I wrote a few words to the Honorable Chamber Deputy Fiannaca."

"Fiannaca? But the Honorable Deputy would never deign to listen to me!"

"To you, certainly not. But to me, he would."

The schoolteacher's expression darkened, and he opened his mouth two or three times to say something, but then closed it again.

"What is it?" asked the commendatore.

"Forgive me for asking—and I don't say that just to be polite—please do forgive me, for asking, that is. But won't Don Memè take offense?"

The commendatore's eyes turned ice cold.

"Memè is a fly that's drawn to the piece of shit. Don't you worry about Ferraguto. Tomorrow morning, I want you to get on the five o'clock train for Misilmesi. It gets in at seven-thirty. At eight, you go knock on the Honorable Fiannaca's door, and he'll see you right away."

"What did you write in that letter?"

"Nothing. I wrote that you are a person of merit who has suffered an injustice, and that you're a friend of mine."

At 8:00 a.m. sharp, Minicuzzo Adornato found himself in the waiting room of the Honorable Paolino Fiannaca, Juris Doctor, deputy of the Chamber, in Misilmesi. As soon as he appeared, Fiannaca—very tall and very thin, with a Tartar mustache, wild eyes behind his pince-nez, and wearing a housecoat and slippers—raised his arms and extended them as if to keep a distance between himself and Minicuzzo.

"Excuse me, but some sort of introduction is needed. The letter from your friend Restuccia wasn't specific. To whom do you wish to speak?"

Minicuzzo gave him a bewildered look. He had woken up very early that morning, and his thoughts were confused.

"I would like to speak—"

"With Fiannaca the lawyer?" the other quickly interrupted him.

"With Fiannaca, yes, but not the lawyer," said Adornato, recovering some of his lucidity.

"With Fiannaca the deputy of the Chamber, then?"

Minicuzzo remained unsure. Fiannaca decided to help him out.

"Is it a political matter?"

"No, sir. At least, I don't think so."

The politician's face brightened.

"So you wish to speak with Fiannaca, the president of the Honor and Family Mutual Aid Association?"

"That's the one," said Adornato, who wasn't so stupid.

"In that case, we need to change venues. This is the Honorable Deputy's study."

He brandished a little key he had drawn from the many hanging on the wall and gestured to Minicuzzo to follow him. Dressed as he was, Fiannaca went out the front door and turned right. He walked past a small door beside which was an enameled plaque with the words PAOLO FIANNACA, LAWYER, and in front of which stood five or six people who bowed reverently and murmured greetings and blessings as the politician passed. A few yards down was another small door with another plaque, which read: HONOR AND FAMILY MUTUAL AID ASSOCIATION. Leaning against the doorjamb was a man six and a half feet tall in hunter's dress, rifle on his shoulder, cartridge belt strapped around his belly.

"Give it to me," he said, as soon as Fiannaca came within range.

The politician handed him the key, and the man opened the door, went inside, and threw open the window in the spacious, lone room that served as the headquarters of the Mutual Aid Association.

"Need anything else, Ixcillincy?"

"No, nothing. Just wait outside."

Aside from some ten chairs, two desks—behind one of which Fiannaca sat down—and a few oil lamps, the big room had no furnishings. There was not a single sheet of paper, folder, or binder to be seen anywhere. Apparently, all agreements were strictly verbal at this association.

"My dear friend Restuccia wrote me that you have suffered an injustice. So why, then, did you not appeal to justice?"

"Because if justice itself does an injustice, it cannot turn around and screw itself by doing justice."

"Logical enough," said the politician. "So you've been done an injustice?"

"No, your honor, my father has. He was accused of theft and arrested by order of the prefect Bortuzzi."

"Ah," Fiannaca commented drily.

"And the prefect came up with this charge of theft only because my father doesn't like the opera that the prefect arranged to have performed at the new theatre of Vigàta.

He's also involved Captain Villaroel and Don Memè Ferra-guto in the matter."

"Stop right there," the suddenly attentive politician enjoined him. Then he shouted: "Gaetanino!"

The hunter materialized at once, as if by magic trick.

"What is it?"

"Please repeat to Gaetanino what you just said to me."

Minicuzzo felt overcome with anger. What did these two want from him? Was it a threat?

"I'd even repeat it before Christ. The prefect sent my father to jail by setting a trap for him with the complicity of Captain Villaroel and that great big sonofabitch Don Memè Ferraguto."

"Did I hear correctly?" Fiannaca asked calmly. "Did you just call Don Memè a sonofabitch?"

Minicuzzo realized that his own life, his father's, and that of his entire family hung on the answer he would give to this question. He summoned a courage he didn't know he possessed, and it was this discovery, more than the tension, that made him sweat.

"Yessir. Don Memè is a great big sonofabitch."

The politician eyed him for a moment, then turned to the hunter.

"Gaetanino, you heard him with your own ears. This gentleman, who was recommended to me by Commendator Restuccia, is one of us. From this moment on, if, for example, he goes outside on a rainy day and slips on a wet spot, I don't want him to touch the ground; I want there to be someone beside him who will catch him in midair. Have I made myself clear?"

"Perfectly."

Gaetanino brought two fingers to his cap and went out.

"And now to us," said Fiannaca. "Let's start again from the beginning. I've been away from Sicily for three months; I'm always busy at parliament. And all I've heard so far on this matter have been rumors, about which, to be honest, I haven't understood a damned thing. Would you please explain to me what's going on in Vigàta?"

↝

At around three in the afternoon, Don Memè was watching people posting the bills announcing the forthcoming opera performance on the walls of Vigàta, so enraged that smoke and flames seemed to be coming out of his nostrils. He was upset because, while in Montelusa and the nearby towns the bills remained in place, in Vigàta they were gone in less than half an hour without anyone's knowing what had become of them. Thus Don Memè had taken to following the posting (the third! Sons of bitches!) in person until the glue began to take, because once the glue dried, it would become much more difficult for those so inclined to tear away the bills. At one point his concentration on the posters' efforts was distracted by a trotting horse that pulled up beside him. Don Memè raised his head and saw that the horse's rider was Gaetanino Sparma, field watcher for the Honorable Fiannaca of Misilmesi. Field watcher in a manner of speaking, that is, because it was known to one and all that, first, Gaetanino couldn't tell the difference between an olive tree and a grapevine, and, second, the Honorable Fiannaca didn't have so much as a kitchen garden. It was a euphemism: it meant that Sparma was employed in the other "fields" in which Fiannaca was involved. And Don Memè knew this very well.

"Don Gaetanino! What a pleasure! What brings you to these parts?"

"Just passing through, and in a hurry."

"Come down for a minute and let me buy you a glass of wine."

The other dismounted, still holding the rifle on his shoulder, and they vigorously shook hands.

"You'll have to forgive me, Don Memè, for not accepting, but I really don't have the time. I was just passing through."

And he didn't say another word, but only readjusted the reins. Don Memè suddenly realized that things were serious indeed, and that it was up to him to speak.

"Is there anything wrong? The Honorable—"

"The Honorable Fiannaca," the other interrupted, "told me just this morning that if I had the pleasure of running into you, I was to tell you something."

"I await your orders."

"Orders? Just the humblest of requests. The Honorable Deputy wants you to know that a mistake was surely made in that matter involving the carpenter who was arrested. A mistake on your part, Don Memè."

"Oh, yeah?"

"Yes. And being too friendly with the prefect is also a mistake."

Don Memè turned pale.

"I'd like to explain," he began.

The other looked at him, cold as ice.

"To me? You want to explain things to me? I don't understand the first thing about these matters. I only do what I'm told. If you've got anything to explain, you'll have to explain it to the Honorable Deputy."

He got back on his horse in one bound and set off at a gallop without saying so much as good-bye.

♦♦♦

After Don Memè, pale but determined, frantically recounted all this to the Lumìas, husband and wife, the signora sent for Captain Villaroel. Pale in turn, but equally determined, she explained to the captain how Saint Anthony had appeared to her in a dream and enlightened her, bringing her memory back. It was she herself who had hidden the jewels, afraid that a new maid might steal them, and then she had completely forgotten about it. They had to take immediate action. An innocent man such as the carpenter, wrongly accused, must not be allowed to spend another minute in prison. She was ready to pay damages for the false accusation.

♦♦♦

"I'm so delighted your innocence was rehognized," Bortuzzi said to the trembling old man standing in front of him. "But before you go home, I would like to ask you something of no importance."

"I'm your humble servant," the carpenter managed to mutter.

"Would you be so hind as to explain to me why you were so against the staging of *The Brewer of Preston* in Vigàta?"

The carpenter gave him a befuddled look. He was ready for anything except that question, and he became convinced that the prefect was actually deigning to joke around with someone like him.

"Do you mean that seriously, sir?"

"Huite seriously, my friend."

The carpenter thought it over for a moment; then, feeling reassured, he began.

"Excellency, I was born in eighteen hundred and five. My father was poor, and sometimes we went hungry in our house. The moment I turned six, I was taken on as a helper by Foderà the carpenter, who was a distant relative of my mother's. Foderà was a master woodworker known all over Palermo, a real artist. He began to grow fond of me, and took me everywhere with him. Once, when I was about ten, Master Foderà took me to the palazzo of a German man who went by the name of Marsan, I think, and who needed some minor repairs done on two antique armoires. But the German was very jealously protective of his furniture, and he insisted that the work be done in his palazzo, even if this cost him more. And since he liked to come and watch us while we worked, he sometimes played his flute in the same room we were working in. One day a baron by the name of Pisani paid him a call. This baron kept talking about how, a few years before, he had gone to the Real Teatro Carolino and heard an opera that I think was called *Fannu tutte accussì* by a certain Mozzat, and that although this opera had seemed magnficent to him, no one else in Palermo had liked it. And so the baron had made up his mind to bring another opera by this same Mozzat to Palermo, the one called *U flautu magicu*, and all at his expense. He had the singers, orchestra, décor, and everything else brought from Naples, paying it all out of his own pocket. Anyway, the baron told the German that the following day there was going to be this performance and that he didn't want anyone else from Palermo in the theatre, only the German. I still don't know why, at that moment, I dropped what I was working on, planted myself in front of Mr. Marsan, and asked him if I could also come to the performance. The German started laughing, and then he looked at the baron, who nodded yes. The next day, there were only the three of us in the theatre: the baron and Mr. Marsan sat in the biggest box, and I went all the way up, near the roof. After the orchestra had been playing and the singers singing for barely five minutes, I'm sure I must have had a high fever. My heart was beating fast, and I felt really hot one minute, and really cold the next, and my head was spinning. Then I sort of turned into a soap bubble, the light and transparent kind that little kids blow with straws for fun, and I started to fly. Yessir, that's right, to fly. You've got to believe me, Excellency. I was flying! And the first thing I saw was the theatre, from the outside, then the piazza with all the people and animals in it, then the whole city, which looked really tiny to me, and then green countrysides, the great rivers of the North, the yellow deserts they say are in Africa, and then I saw the whole world, a little ball colored like an egg yolk. After that I came close to the sun, and I went even higher and ended up in heaven among the clouds and fresh air all painted light blue and some stars that were still shining. Then the singing and music ended; I reopened my eyes and saw that I was now alone in the theatre. I didn't want to go outside. I could still hear the music inside me. I fell asleep, and then I woke up, fainted, and then came to again; I laughed and I cried, I was born and I died, with the music playing inside me all the while. The next day, still feverish, I asked Mr. Marsan to teach me how to play the flute, and he did. And that's the story, Your Excellency. Ever since that day I go to hear concerts and operas, sometimes I even take the train, and I'm always looking and looking, but I can never find what I'm looking for."

"What are you loohing for?" asked the prefect, who had risen to his feet without realizing it.

"For some music, Excellency, that will make me feel as happy as I did then, that will let me see what the heavens are like. Now, this *Brewer*, Your Excellency, is probably all right, as music goes, I won't say it's not, but—"

"Never mind," Bortuzzi said brusquely.

An ordinary-looking young man

An ordinary-looking young man presented himself at Puglisi's office at around three o'clock in the afternoon, when the lieutenant's cojones were still smoking from the words he had exchanged with Dr. Gammacurta's son half an hour earlier.

~~~

"But why were neither you nor your mother worried when your father didn't come home last night?"

"Mamà was convinced that my father had gone to spend the night with that whore of a midwife, as he often did."

"All right, but I know that when the doctor did not go to see her during the night, and didn't show up at his office in the morning, the midwife, not the whore, as you call her, got worried and even came to your house to ask if Dr. Gammacurta was sick. Is this true or not?"

"Yes, it's true, the whore came to our place."

"And?"

"Mamà told the whore that wherever my father happened to be was of no concern to a whore like her."

"But, good God, if your father was missing—since even the wh—, I mean the midwife, was worried about him—how come you didn't race down here to tell me you had no news of him?"

"Excuse me, Lieutenant, but if my mother and I had first come to you, let's say, at the crack of dawn this morning, would my father have been saved?"

"No. When I found him he was still alive, but he'd already lost too much blood."

"And so?"

Puglisi pounded his fist on the table, hurting his hand, cursed the saints, got up from his chair, circled twice around the room, and finally felt calmer.

"Excuse me, Lieutenant, but what's this behavior of yours supposed to mean?"

"Son, it means that your father was absolutely right to get shot, seeing that he was condemned to live in the company of people like you and your mother. Good day."

⌇⌇

The ordinary-looking young man who entered the office after Gammacurta's son had left did not seem so ordinary to Puglisi the moment he said a few words.

"My name is Mario Filastò," said the lad, "and I'm a specialist with the Property Insurers' Association of Palermo."

Puglisi looked at him. The young man was wearing a rumpled suit with a torn pocket hanging from the jacket, and his hands and face were blackened with soot. Filastò immediately noticed the policeman's curiosity.

"I apologize for the state I'm in, but I got all dirty when I was inspecting the theatre."

"And how do I look?" Puglisi countered brusquely, not having managed to change his clothes, which, after being soaked with wet salt, were now clinging to his body as they began to dry, solidifying as if they were made of quick-drying cement.

"You see, sir, the moment I arrived in Vigàta, everybody told me the theatre caught fire by accident, perhaps from somebody dropping a still-burning cigar. But if what people are saying is right, then the company I represent will have to pay for the damages—there's no getting around it, just like when you play blackjack. But if they're wrong, and the theatre was set on fire deliberately, then that changes everything and my company is no longer required to pay so much as a counterfeit sou. Do you see what I'm saying?"

"I see what you're saying. And what do you yourself think?"

"I think the theatre was set on fire deliberately."

"You're supposed to think that way, if you don't mind my saying so, because, if you can prove what you think, you'll save your company a pile of money. The problem is that what you think is not enough."

"Actually, sir, I don't think anything. I have a firm conviction that is borne out by certain facts. Believe me, we have a criminal case on our hands. That's why I came to see you, to ask you to come to the theatre with me. There's something I want to show you. You'll see that what I'm saying is not just hot air."

"Right now?"

"Right now," was young Filastò's implacable reply.

~~~

A peasant-drenching rain was falling, the kind whose fine little drops make it seem as if it's hardly raining at all, and so the peasant keeps working in his field until evening and in the end comes home more drenched than after the Great Flood. As the two men were heading to the theatre, Puglisi felt his clothes softening, his trousers now allowing him a smoother step.

"Take my word for it," said Filastò. "I have a lot of experience with fire. I know how it starts, how it grows, how whimsical it can be, how the slightest thing is enough to change its mind, its direction, or its strength. The fire in the theatre started at the rear of the building, not in the auditorium where the people were."

"I've got a vague idea of my own as to where the fire started," said Puglisi.

They arrived in front of the little door leading to the understage. It was all burnt up, the black and white marks of the flames extending onto the wall above the door frame.

"The fire, as we can see, was blowing from here," said the insurance inspector. "And this is where it started. Then it turned halfway around and began attacking the back of the stage. From there it moved on towards the auditorium. Exactly the opposite of what people think. Whoever started the fire also broke the panes of the transom windows to get a better airflow. You see, Lieutenant? The shattered glass fell into the understage area, not outside. Now follow me."

They entered, descending the stairs that had survived the blaze. Once inside, Filastò lit an oil lamp he had set down at the foot of the stairs during his earlier inspection.

"Look here," he said, pointing to a spot right beside the small door. "Here the stagehands said there were a number of rolled-up backdrops that had been placed near the door, ready to be taken outside and loaded after the performance. Look. What are these shards of clay, in your opinion?"

"I dunno, they look like remnants of a jug or a pitcher. Definitely something to hold drinking water."

"No, sir, you're wrong. Follow me."

The young man set down the lamp, dropped into a crouch, and started putting the pieces of earthenware in order, fitting them together. When he had finished, he held in his hands a clay object that threatened to fall back to pieces at any moment. He turned to Puglisi.

"It's not a jug or a pitcher. It's not made for holding water. Have a good look."

"It's a money box, a piggy bank," Puglisi said in amazement.

"Right," said Filastò. "And there are other pieces from a second money box over there, where the opera troupe's costumes were kept."

"It certainly seems odd that everyone in the troupe would suddenly feel like saving money," commented Puglisi, who didn't know what to make of it.

Filastò let the pieces of the money box fall back onto the floor. Two remained in his hands, and he thrust these under Puglisi's nose.

"Smell," he said.

Puglisi brought his nose closer and inhaled. A wrinkle appeared on his brow.

"Smells like kerosene," he said.

"And would you believe me if I said that the other pieces of the second piggy bank also smell like kerosene?"

"I would. What does it mean?"

Filastò didn't answer. He put the two fragments down and wiped his hands on his suit, whose original color was now lost to the world.

"Is there anyone in town who makes or sells ceramics?"

"Yes, there's Don Pitrino."

"Let's go pay him a call."

"While we're at it," said Puglisi, resigned, throwing his hands up.

On their way there, the lieutenant felt he should compliment the young man.

"You certainly have to have an eye to realize that those shards were not from something that was broken during the fire."

"Yes, you have to have an eye for it. But it's like a game, a challenge. You look at all the damage caused by the fire, you look very carefully, and then you look again and you say: there's something here that doesn't add up. And so you look yet again, until you finally find what it is that doesn't add up."

Zu Pitrino, who liked Puglisi, greeted the policeman with a smile.

"My friend here," said Puglisi, "would like to buy a piggy bank for his little boy."

"I've got 'em in all sizes."

"He's interested in one about so big." And he held out his hands to show the size.

"I've got half a dozen that size," said the old man. "Come out to the yard."

Behind the little house, the yard was crammed full of jugs and pitchers big and small, carafes, amphorae, vases, pots, and roof tiles. As the old man was showing them where the piggy banks were lined up, he suddenly froze, speechless.

"What's wrong?" asked Puglisi.

"What's wrong is that yesterday afternoon I counted the

piggy banks like your friend wants, and there was six of 'em, and now there's only four. See the empty space there, and the two little circles where they were? I guess some son of a whore jumped the fence last night and stole 'em."

Filastò and Puglisi exchanged a quick glance of understanding. The old man bent down to pick up one of the four remaining banks.

"This one all right?"

It was all right. Filastò then asked him to fill the piggy bank with kerosene, which was among the items one could buy in the old man's shop. Although it was an odd request, Zu Pitrino asked no questions and did as he was told, but not without some difficulty. Filastò also asked him for a piece of cloth. Puglisi paid and they both left. Some ten paces from the old man's house, they were already in the open country. Filastò then gave the lieutenant a practical demonstration of how the combination of piggy bank, kerosene, and rag worked.

As they walked away, the grass, twigs, and brush that the young man had piled up behind them were still burning from the piggy bank he had crashed against them, despite the fact that they were all sodden with rain.

"How did you figure it out?"

"You mean how the two piggy banks were used this way? I didn't figure it out myself, I merely remembered something. Our insurance company is a big firm. It has offices all over Italy, and these offices exchange information on the many different ways people manage to screw their insurers. I recalled that our agent in Naples and another in Rome had brought to our attention a couple of cases where—"

"In Rome, you say?" Puglisi interrupted, suddenly very attentive.

"Yes, in Naples and in Rome."

"Sorry, but I would like your opinion on something. Why do you think they set fire to the theatre?"

"Bah, I wouldn't know. Maybe because there are some people in Vigàta who want to screw the prefect more than the prefect has managed to screw himself."

"Sorry again, but are you really convinced that the fire broke out a few hours after everything was over and people had already gone home? Let me rephrase that: after more than the reasonably plausible amount of time needed for an accidental fire to catch and grow?"

"There's no doubt about it: the fire was started from scratch, a few hours after calm had returned to Vigàta."

"I'm not convinced."

"Of what?"

"That some Vigatese, after everything had calmed down, would have second thoughts like a cornuto and set fire to the theatre. That's not the way people do things here. This was done by an outsider."

Back in the center of town, Filastò took leave of Puglisi.

"I'm going back to the theatre to look for more evidence. So you agree, in principle, that it was a case of arson?'

"I do."

They exchanged a look of sympathy and said good-bye. Puglisi then turned his back and practically started running towards police headquarters.

"Saddle my horse, quick," he said upon entering.

∿

Halfway to Montelusa, with the rain coming down hard again, he fell off his horse from fatigue, got his clothes even dirtier, hurt his shoulder, climbed back into the saddle, and resumed galloping as fast as the sodden ground would allow the beast to go. At the commissariat everyone looked at him in curiosity and bewilderment because of the state he was in, and even Dr. Meli, "*u tabbutu*"—or, "the tomb"—said aloud what the others had been thinking but hadn't expressed.

"You'd better not let the commissioner see you in that condition."

"Well, then you can talk to the commissioner on my behalf."

"I should warn you that the commissioner is quite irritated at you for the note you sent him. You asked for three days to conduct the investigation, which is fine, but you added that the investigation might end up implicating some 'highly placed individuals.' Does this seem like the sort of thing you should set down so carelessly in black and white?"

Puglisi's anger flared.

"All right, since you bring it up, I want you to tell the commissioner that when I wrote 'highly placed individuals,' I used the plural to give myself a wide berth, but in fact I was thinking only of the prefect. Now I'm convinced that I was right to use the plural."

"So you think other individuals are implicated?"

"Yessir."

"Such as?"

"Such as the person you're going to talk to in a few moments."

Dr. Meli leapt straight into the air—actually leapt, so that when he came back down, one of the windowpanes rattled. He turned pale, violently seized Puglisi's arm, brought his face close, and hissed:

"Do you realize what you're saying?"

"Perfectly. Why didn't you order me to arrest the Mazzinian from Rome at once?"

"Silence!" Meli commanded. "Come into my office!"

They left the antechamber, where the caravan of people who had been coming and going were suddenly all ears. Once inside the office, Puglisi, without waiting to be asked, collapsed into a chair, exhausted.

"Explain yourself. But try to remain calm and don't raise your voice."

"Why didn't you give me a warrant to arrest the Mazzinian from Rome at once?" Puglisi asked again, having calmed down a little.

"I explained the matter to the commissioner."

"And?"

"He told me to wait a few days, at least until after the inauguration of the theatre."

"Why?"

"I don't know what to tell you."

"What a brilliant idea on the commissioner's part! If they had let me arrest him in time, it's possible he would never have managed to burn down the theatre!"

"Are you convinced it was him?"

"I'm not yet certain. But as soon as I get my hands on him, I'm going to make him tell me everything, and you'll see that I'm right. Give me the warrant, in writing and dated."

Meli rose very slowly, as if his bottom were stuck to the chair, went and knocked on the commissioner's door, and entered.

"Cavaliere, Puglisi's in my office."

"What's he want?"

"He wants an immediate warrant for the arrest of that Mazzinian hiding out in Vigàta, Traquandi."

"Let him have it."

"All right, sir, but the problem is that the lieutenant thinks that Traquandi is the person who set fire to the theatre."

"So?"

"Cavaliere, if it was the Roman who did it, and Puglisi is seldom wrong, we'll be blamed by Puglisi himself for not having arrested him sooner."

"Oh, shit!" said the commissioner, having finally understood.

"And there are even two deaths in the mix."

"Weren't there three?"

"Yessir, but the third death, that of Dr. Gammacurta, is not on our account. He was shot by Villaroel's men. He goes onto the prefect's account."

The commissioner looked at Meli, then batted his eyelashes and made an inquisitive face.

"Listen, Meli, are you really so sure that it was I who gave the order to delay the arrest? Might it not be possible that you misunderstood what I said to you?"

It was an old story, but this time Meli would have none of it. The risk was too great.

"I'm sorry, Cavaliere, but this time I remember the circumstances very clearly, because the scrivener had already drafted the arrest warrant and I told him to tear it up, after you had decided otherwise."

The cavaliere had tried. He changed tactic.

"What can we do?"

"Think it over a moment before receiving Puglisi."

The moment of reflection turned into two hours of whispered words and long, thoughtful silences, to the point that when Dr. Meli finally went to call Puglisi for his meeting with the commissioner, he found him asleep, his head on the table, arms dangling beside his legs.

If on a winter's night already

If on a winter's night already fraught with wind and rain and thunder and lightning a traveler had passed through the piazza in which Vigàta's new theatre stood and seen the damage around him—the upended street lamps, ruined flower beds, broken glass, mounted soldiers patrolling the streets, carriages racing back and forth with the injured and ladies who had fainted—and heard the distant gunshots, the voices shouting in pain or anger, crying for help or cursing, he would have spurred his horse and headed quickly away from what he would have rightly believed to be a new '48. Never would he have imagined that all that havoc, all that devastation, had been caused by a soprano who had hit a false note. A ghastly, horrendous note, to be sure, one that had sounded to all as if a steamship had entered the theatre and blasted its foghorn, to say nothing of the fact that someone else had fired a carbine at the same moment. But what had really triggered the general stampede was the skill of the man who had built the theatre. A theatre—reasoned the architect—should be constructed so that the people in the audience can hear everything that is sung or played or said onstage. Thus, added to the steamship horn and gunshot was a rumble at once earthquake-like and yet harmonious, arising from some unknown part of the theatre. If one had thought about it with a cool head—which certainly wasn't possible at that moment of pandemonium—the explanation for that sound could have been found in the fact that among everything and everyone else in the theatre there were also the orchestra musicians, who, after hearing the gunshot and the siren blast (not necessarily in that order), and being understandably on edge from the way the evening was going, decided all at once to free themselves of their instruments, the better to run away. Now, there were so many of these instruments—from double basses, bassoons, and trombones to violins and piccolos to kettledrums and snares—that, when tossed into the air and then striking the ground, they made a tremendous noise, having been dropped in that part of the theatre called the "pit," the purpose of which is to amplify the orchestra's sound—which it certainly did, having no way of knowing that the sound, on that occasion, was not music, and the result of which was that it suddenly sounded to everyone, for no reason whatsoever, as if the theatre had decided to sink into the earth.

Don Memè Ferraguto hadn't budged either when the soprano hit her false note or when the carbine went off; but when he heard that magical, disturbing sound rise up from beneath the stage, he felt his blood curdle.

"It's a bomb!" he cried.

Grabbing the prefect's wife, who was sitting there dumbfounded, he lifted her bodily and carried her to the rear of the box, where he propped her up against the wall, during which time Captain Villaroel, at a loss as to what was happening, violently unsheathed his sword. The mayor, whose reflexes were a tad slow, had the misfortune of rising from his

seat and straight into the path of the captain's sword. He fell
backwards, forehead cleft by the tip of the blade, but no one
took any notice of him. The prefect, for his part, was more
quickly on his feet and at his wife's side, thus benefiting in
part from Don Memè's protection.

Such was the situation when people began to try to leave
the orchestra and boxes and encountered the resistance of the
militiamen, who repelled them with kicks and blows with the
flat of their swords. Their orders were to allow nobody to
leave, and they were following those orders. It was during this
confusion of pushing and pulling that Don Artemisio Laganà,
well known until that moment as a man of serene disposition
always ready for reasonable negotiation, suddenly lost his head
and prudent sense of judgment and pulled out his sword stick,
the blade hidden inside his cane, and skewered the shoulder of
one militiaman by the name of Arfio Tarantino while at the
same time shouting, for reasons unknown:

"Charge!"

Never in his life had Signor Artemisio Laganà so much as
worn a soldier's uniform, and yet on that occasion the tone of
voice that emerged from his chest was that of a man-at-arms
accustomed to combat. Thus the soldierly command, uttered
with such force that it could be heard all the way up in the
gallery, had the effect of spurring the mob to battle, and in a
certain methodical order, against the militiamen blocking
the exit.

The women, whom the men at first had chivalrously let
go ahead of them towards the exit, were quickly pulled back,
so to speak, to the rear lines, while the strongest lads and the
men most ready to give it their all went on the attack. Here
it should also be added that Corporal Vito Caruana, when

ordered not to let a living soul out of the theatre, had got it
in his head to lock both rows of boxes, since the key to each
box was hanging on the door outside. And thus the occupants of the boxes had no choice, for a while, but to try to
break down the doors, which, however, put up a solid resistance. The situation of all those in the orchestra and gallery,
was, of course, entirely different, since they naturally didn't
have to knock down any doors; on the other hand, they
found themselves pitted alone against the armed militiamen.
The people in the first row of boxes, meanwhile, having discovered after a few attempts that the doors would not open,
realized that they needed only to climb over the railings and
leap a short distance to reach the open space of the orchestra
below them. And so they jumped, helping one another and
lowering women and old folks into each other's arms. Once
the evacuation was completed, the youngest among them
rushed to lend a hand to the people in the orchestra trying to
get out.

In the gallery, on the other hand, things were taking a
different turn. At the blast of the carbine, the blare of the
foghorn, and the terrifying, mysterious rumble that followed,
Lollò Sciacchitano and his friend Sciaverio automatically
found themselves shoulder to shoulder, as was always their
custom in tavern brawls. Heads turned one towards the other,
they looked each other in the eye and settled on a plan of
action without saying a word. Slowly advancing towards a
soldier who watched them without moving, they broke into
a run when about two paces away from him and charged
forward screaming very loudly. In terror, the soldier raised
his carbine and took aim. At this point the two turned their
backs to him and, still screaming like madmen, started

running in the opposite direction. Instinctively, the soldier gave chase, and that was what did him in: Sciacchitano suddenly stopped, but Sciaverio kept on running and the militiaman ran after him. It was too late when he realized he'd been tricked, as Sciacchitano, right behind him, dealt him a fierce chop to the nape of the neck with the side of his hand, and the soldier dropped to the ground like an empty sack. A second soldier who found himself face-to-face with the two met a similar fate but by different means. Sciacchitano and Sciaverio jumped on him and started shoving, and the soldier started pushing back in turn. When the trio found themselves in a stalemate, the two friends suddenly pulled one step back, and the militiaman, carried by the force of his own thrust, fell face forward to the floor. Sciaverio kicked him in the head, dispatching him to dreamland, removed his carbine, and even took six bullets from his ammunition belt. The four remaining soldiers gave in to the pressure of the gallery gods, with one falling backwards and rolling down the stairs, and the other three stepping aside as the mob hurtled down to the entrance lobby.

In the second row of boxes, the situation seemed to have stabilized, to the point where Captain Villaroel carefully opened the door to the royal box and looked in: there were no people in the corridor. Corporal Caruana, the only soul around, came up to him.

"Everything's in order here, Captain, sir. They're unable to leave the boxes because I locked them in and the doors are strong. What should I do?"

"Go downstairs with your men and give a hand to the troops in the orchestra. I'll stay here and guard His Excellency."

Caruana obeyed, while Villaroel, with sabre still unsheathed, took up position in front of the royal box, eyes on the lookout.

Neither of the two had taken into account the gymnastic skills of one Serafino Uccellatore, a house burglar in his youth and now a respected cordage dealer. When he realized that the people in the second row of boxes were imprisoned, Serafino, then in the orchestra, clambered up to the balustrade of the first row of boxes, straightened himself, regained his balance, grabbed the feet of a wooden statue of a naked woman with wings, dangled in the void for a moment, reached up and clutched the railing of the box overhead, pulled himself up by the strength of his arms, and, flying briefly through the air, landed inside the box, where he was greeted by the applause of those who had been watching his maneuver. Once inside the box, he cocked the revolver he always carried with him, aimed at the lock, and fired. The blast was followed by generalized shouting and an increased surge of the crowd. The door came open. Before his own terrified eyes, Captain Villaroel saw a sort of athlete sprint down the corridor and open all the boxes, door after door, after which the occupants came pouring out, yelling, as in a massive prison break. The soldiers who were defending the two landings that led downstairs had no choice but to step back against the wall and let the escapees pass. At this point, all the townsfolk who had gone to the theatre jammed into the great entrance lobby. Leaving, however, was impossible. One Lieutenant Sileci, who was outside with his soldiers, had had his men place beams of wood through the handles of the large glass-and-wood inner door, so that it could no longer be opened from the inside. And, for good measure, a line of militiamen waited with their carbines pointed menacingly at the lobby. Smothered by the press of bodies, three or four ladies fainted and had to be laid down on the floor. And just as Don Artemisio Laganà had, in a sense, taken military command of the situation, Headmaster Cozzo likewise informally declared himself civilian chief.

"All the fainted ladies over here," he ordered.

The people obeyed, and the ladies, some dragged by the ankles, others held by the head and feet and lifted, were piled up in a corner of the lobby.

"Everybody charge! Charge!" Laganà hollered in the meanwhile.

"But there are horses outside!" someone told him.

"And the soldiers are aiming their rifles at us!" another seconded him.

As indecision seemed to take hold in the lobby, Captain Villaroel, unaware of what was happening downstairs, decided he could attempt an exit.

"Everybody out!" he shouted to the occupants of the box.

As the prefect, his wife, Don Memè, and the mayor, who was holding a bloodied handkerchief to his forehead, filed out, they felt deceptively reassured, since there was no sign of anyone around them.

They began descending the staircase, the captain leading the way, sabre drawn, with Don Memè bringing up the rear. When, still on the stairs, they came within sight of the lobby, they found themselves up against a shifting, tempestuous wall of bodies emitting cries and laments. With as strong a voice as he could muster, Villaroel shouted:

"Make way for His Excellency!"

And, just to be sure, he started blindly dealing blows

with the flat of his sword to the left and right. Thus the group was able to go down into the lobby, but, once there, they couldn't take another step either backward or forward. Then, to make matters worse, Villaroel, as he continued to yell and use the flat of his sabre, felt the cold barrel of a carbine pointed directly against the back of his skull. It was the weapon seized by Sciaverio.

"Throw down the sword, asshole!"

Villaroel obeyed, and immediately Laganà took possession of his weapon.

"Charge! Charge!" he repeated, brandishing the sword and passing his sword stick to a gentleman beside him.

Seeing that pandemonium was breaking out, Don Memè wisely brought the prefect and his wife into a corner and shielded them with his body. Meanwhile Sciaverio, just to do something new, fired a shot of his carbine into the theatre's inner door, shattering the glass and eliciting more loud screams from the crowd.

Amidst all the confusion, Don Tanino Licalzi, known as "Lightfingers" for his bad habit of groping with near-superhuman skill the bottoms of all the women who came within reach, was able, in the darkness, confusion, and press, to amass such a hoard of gropes that his right hand began to ache. And yet at a certain point he became obsessed with the fact that his collection was still missing the bottom of *la signora prefettessa*. So he did and said what he needed to do, maneuvering his way through the tumultuous throng, and at last found himself right beside the prefect's wife. Closing his eyes in a foretaste of pleasure, he reached out, encountered a silk-covered buttock, and squeezed.

"Someone is touching my bottom!" the prefectess screamed in dismay and indignation, and with a hint of glee.

Having achieved his goal, Don Tanino fell to his knees and pretended to faint. But the lady's cry had touched the heart and honor of Don Memè, who, wild with rage over the sacrilegious act, snatched his revolver from his jacket pocket and fired three shots into the air.

"Stand back! Stand back!" he cried in a sputtering voice.

At the sound of the shots, the nearest people stepped away and a small space cleared around Don Memè, the prefect, and his wife, who continued to mutter:

"Somebody touched my bottom!"

Hearing the three pistol shots, Headmaster Cozzo decided to take action. This time he drew his revolver in earnest, after years of practice. Finger on the trigger, he thought about it for a moment, tasting a hint of lemon in his mouth, and then fired. The bullet—happy to be free after decades of confinement—treated itself to a flight itinerary that would have driven a ballistics expert mad. After striking the ceiling of the lobby, it shot off towards a wall and hit the side of the bronze bas-relief representing the face of Maestro Agenore Zummo (1800–1870), eminent head of the Vigàta Music Circle. Upon nicking Maestro Zummo's right eye, the bullet headed towards the vast central chandelier, grazed a copper pinnacle, and, following a parabolic trajectory, ended up stuck just under the skin of the occiput of the mayor, who was still unable to stanch the flow of blood from his forehead. Newly injured, the mayor let out a squeal like a slaughtered pig and fell straight to the floor, breaking his nose.

Still at a loss as to what he was doing, Sciaverio, hiding behind the broad bottoms of three ladies who had fainted and were piled one atop the other, fired another random shot of the carbine. At this point Lieutenant Sileci and his horse leapt into the open space that had formed around Don Memè and his two charges. The lieutenant had had the inner door opened by his soldiers, who nevertheless remained on guard to prevent people from exiting. The jump he executed was truly for the annals of horsemanship, something he had learned not at riding school but during his fraternal association with a fugitive brigand whom he used to visit in the bush during his free time, for fun and friendship and common business interests. Sileci bent down from the horse, grabbed the prefectess by the arm, and put her in front of him in the saddle, then seized the prefect, hoisted him up, and put him in the saddle behind him. Then he spurred his horse to make it leap yet again and turn back. This time, however, the beast, weighed down as it was, couldn't manage it.

At that very moment Headmaster Cozzo, literally in the throes of ecstasy over having successfully fired his revolver, got off a second shot right behind the horse's ears. Terrorized, the creature leapt over the entire throng and ended up outside the theatre. With the help of the militiamen, Sileci put the prefectess and prefect in their carriage and sent them off to Montelusa under an escort of four of his men.

The passage of Sileci's horse, however, had inevitably opened a momentary breach in the line of militiamen outside, and the crowd took advantage of this, spilling suddenly out into the open, just as the lights in the square were going out. What had happened, in fact, was that a handful of young men from the town, to help their fellow townsfolk trapped inside the theatre, had decided that the darkness of the night would be their friend, and so, tying three street lamps with cables to three horses, they had uprooted them. Whereupon, for no reason and without being ordered to, the soldiers began to attack the people who were running away in the piazza and on the streets. And still other things happened. Such as when Sciaverio, pursued by a militiaman, fired a shot that hit the soldier in the hand, or when a militiaman named Francesco Miccichè, in pursuit of another civilian, entered a very narrow alleyway and received a chamber-pot full of shit and piss on his head.

Lieutenant Puglisi did not take part in any phase of the battle. At the start of the mayhem he had sat down in a seat in the orchestra and buried his head in his hands.

It was a pleasure to set the fire

*I*t was a pleasure to set the fire, no doubt about it. But then to see
it grow, climb higher and higher, spreading outwards, eating everything in its path as it sang, little by little the pleasure turned to joy
and I was as hard as if I was fucking.

"I gotta try that again," Traquandi said to himself, strip-
ping down naked and lying belly-up, as he nearly always did
when he wanted to facilitate the onset of sleep.

In the cot beside his, Decu had already been sleeping
soundly for the past hour, his breathing long and regular, as
if he were singing a lullaby to himself.

᭜

The following night they were awakened by an insistent
knocking at the door. The knocking was not so hard as to
seem like a command; rather, it was more like a request to
enter. But it sufficed, when the two awoke with a start, to make
their blood run cold.

"Hold it, don't open," Traquandi ordered Decu, realizing
that the other was about to light a candle, and he grabbed the
rifle his friend had given him, which he had placed by the
head of the bed.

Decu got up slowly, without making any noise, and

the Roman did the same. They positioned themselves on either side of the door, as the knocking continued, polite but firm.

"Who's there?" said Decu, trying to sound self-assured.

"Iss me, Decu, your cousin Girlando."

"Who the hell is it?" asked the Roman.

"It's my cousin, the son of my father's brother."

"What's he want at this hour?"

"I dunno. I'll ask him."

There was no need, since the man behind the door continued:

"Open up, Decu, I need to talk to you. To you and the young Roman who's there with you."

Traquandi literally jumped, nervously clutching the rifle he held in his now-sweaty hands.

"How the fuck does he know I'm here? This is starting to smell fishy to me."

"Calm down!" Decu replied. "If he knows you're hiding out with me, it means they also know at the commissariat of Montelusa."

All at once things became clear to Traquandi.

"You mean you're telling me the guy out there is a cop?"

"Yes. But mostly he's my cousin."

"And what do you mean by 'mostly'?"

"I mean that in these parts that means something."

"Think about it," said the voice outside. "If I wanted to catch you, I would have caught you. You were both sleeping like babies. But not only do I have no intention of catching you, there's no way I could. I'm alone and unarmed. And anyway, Decuzzo, have I ever betrayed you?"

It was these last words that made up Decu's mind.

"We can trust him," he said softly to Traquandi. Then, loudly: "I'll open the door for you in a minute."

The Roman quickly got dressed as Decu lit a lamp and went to open up.

In the doorway stood a squat man with arms raised, his right hand holding a lantern that shed light on a ruddy, friendly face, that of a man well-disposed towards the world as it was, with its people, trees, and animals.

"Greetings, Decuzzo," he said, smiling. "Can I come in?"

Decu didn't answer but stepped aside to let him in, while Traquandi leapt back towards the rear wall, keeping his rifle trained on the new arrival. But the policeman seemed to pay no mind to him. He set his lantern on the floor and sat down on a nearby chair, so that the light shone only on him and his ruddy face, leaving the other two in the cone of shadow, as if to show that he was exposing himself because he had nothing to hide.

"And so?" asked Decu.

"It's all rather complicated," said Girlando. "Complicated to explain and to understand."

"You here to screw me?" came Traquandi's brutal question, unable as he was to understand the formality between the two.

"No," said the cop, raising a hand. "No. On the contrary."

"Then, out with it, cousin!"

"Decu, you may be nervous, but so am I. Because if the commissariat ever finds out that I came here to see you, my career is ruined, to say the least. You have to understand that. We need to talk this over and try to see where things stand. So, to begin: That prick of a prefect of Montelusa decides that the new theatre in Vigàta has to open with a worthless opera. And he gets his way, turning everyone against him. And the opera ends up the way it was supposed to end up, in a pile of shit. Do we all agree on that?"

"We agree," said Decu, a bit thrown off by the fact that his cousin was approaching things in such a roundabout way. He couldn't tell where his cousin was going with this.

"Then what happens?" the cop continued. "What happens is that after everything grows calm again, two hours after the pandemonium in the theatre, the theatre catches fire. And that's strange."

"Why?" asked Traquandi. "Fire takes time to catch. In all the confusion, if somebody dropped a cigar—"

Girlando cut him off with a stare.

"I haven't got any time to waste. If we're just going to bullshit ourselves with this story of a cigar, I'm going to get up and leave."

"All right, all right. Go on," said Decu.

"Everybody knows us Vigatese. And they all know we're capable of doing the worst kinds of things, but always on impulse, in the heat of the moment, face-to-face. We would never do something like this on the sly, two hours after the fact, all nice and rested. We never have second thoughts the way cornuti do. Therefore, whoever burned down the theatre was not from Vigàta, but an outsider. And Lieutenant Puglisi had this exact same idea and went and told it to the commissioner not two hours ago."

"So who does Puglisi think did it?" Decu asked, pallid.

"Puglisi thinks it was the Mazzinian who came here from Rome and who's been in town for the last four days."

"Me?" Traquandi asked huffily.

"Yes, you," said Girlando, eyeing him calmly.

"But even if it was true," Decu cut in, "how would Puglisi prove it?"

"If he ever gets his hands on the gentleman in front of me here," said the cop, "you can bet your family jewels he will make him talk."

He sighed and lit a cigar by the flame of the lamp, letting the others stew in their own juices in the meantime.

"But I'm of another opinion," said Girlando, after taking his first puff on the cigar, as he watched the smoke rise.

The other two clung to these words like castaways to a plank of wood.

"What?" they asked, practically in chorus.

"In my opinion, it was Cocò Impiduglia, the nitwit, the town idiot, who started the fire. Impiduglia can't even talk; he's less than animal. A dog's got more brains than him. And everybody in Vigàta knows there's only one thing that gives him pleasure: setting fire to the first thing he sees. We've arrested him four times: once for setting fire to a straw hut; another time it was a wooden hut. In all good conscience, I think it was him this time, too. Puglisi's wrong."

"If you're so convinced it was that stupid, crazy shit who set fire to the theatre, why'd you come here in the middle of the night to bust our balls?"

Traquandi was anxious. He had taken his handkerchief out of his pocket and was continually wiping his mouth.

"Because it's all very complicated. And I'll explain why. Puglisi is not only convinced that the person who set fire to the theatre, causing two deaths, was the Mazzinian from Rome. He also had the courage to tell the commissioner to his face that if he'd immediately had the Roman arrested, he'd never have had the time or the means to burn down the blessed theatre. And therefore, still in Puglisi's opinion, the commissioner himself is also responsible for the chaos. And that's very serious. Puglisi is a gypsum donkey."

"And what the fuck does that mean?"

"It means he's someone who follows his own path, no matter what happens, even if Samson and all the Philistines die. Understand what I mean?"

"Perfectly," said Decu.

"And so I, on my own, without saying anything to anyone, decided to find a way to set everything right. Since the commissioner gave Puglisi the warrant to arrest the Roman early tomorrow morning, at dawn—in other words, a few hours from now—I dashed over here. If, when he gets here, Puglisi finds you sleeping like an angel all alone, with no sign of the Roman having been in your house, then the whole story becomes a fantasy of Lieutenant Puglisi. There's no proof, no nothing."

"I get it," said Traquandi. "You're saying I gotta clear out of here fast."

"Exactly," said Girlando.

"All right, then. But am I supposed to run away just like that? Where am I gonna go? Where am I gonna run to?"

"Just like that, no. They'd catch up to you in no time, and there would be hell to pay, especially for me, who let you escape."

"So what do we do?"

Girlando paused artfully, extinguishing his cigar butt.

"At the crossroads about a hundred yards from this house, I've got a trusted man of mine waiting for you. His name is Laurentano and he's got two horses, one for you and one for him. If you leave now, without delay, by midmorning you'll already be near Serradifalco, where there's another person of mine who can keep you at his house for three or four days. After which he'll decide himself where to send you."

"So I have to go?"

"Of course you have to go. The arrangement I've made solves everything. Puglisi won't find you, and his idea of who burned down the theatre won't be worth shit. My cousin will deny ever meeting you, and I'll arrest Cocò Impiduglia and persuade him to say what I want him to say, even if it's that he set fire to Rome in Nero's day. That way we can all go on living happily ever after, the commissioner included, like in one of those stories people tell children to help them fall asleep. Believe me, there's no other solution. Think it over, both of you. I'm gonna go outside and get a breath of air."

~~~

They thought it over, discussed it, nearly came to blows, embraced, and made up their minds. Traquandi gathered his belongings, shook Decu's hand, and left in the company of the policeman.

"Stay awake and wait for me, because I need to talk to you," Girlando whispered to Decu before leaving with the Roman.

Less than fifteen minutes later, he returned, visibly content.

"Your Roman friend is in the right hands now. And you should thank me. Because if not for my idea, tomorrow morning you'd be in jail, and it would be very hard to get you out. Two people died, Decu, don't forget that."

"What should I do when Puglisi comes?"

"Don't do anything at all. Or, at the most, get upset, show surprise, start yelling in anger. Meanwhile lemme have this rifle. I don't like the idea of Puglisi finding a firearm in here. I'll throw it into the well as soon as I leave. You have to tell

Puglisi you don't know anything about this Roman, you've never seen him, and, as for the fire at the theatre, you're as innocent as the Baby Jesus. Even if he's so pigheaded that he still arrests you, he'll have no choice but to set you free after half a day. Now gimme some wine; I think I caught a chill."

∿

They walked along a country trail. It was already getting light. All at once Laurentano, a rube like so many of the people Traquandi had met the past few days, addressed the Roman without even turning his head.

"So you're from Rome?"

"From Rome, yes."

"And what's Rome like?"

"Beautiful."

"An' the pope, you ever see 'im?"

Traquandi didn't understand the question.

"What did you say?"

"The pope. You ever see the pope?"

"No. Never seen 'im."

"*Maria santissima!*" Laurentano marveled. "You're from Rome an' you never seen the pope? If I lived in Rome, I'd be there all day every day, on my knees, in front of the church where the pope lives, just waiting to see him so I could ask his forgiveness for all my sins. But you, are you Christian or not?"

Traquandi didn't answer. And Laurentano didn't open his mouth again for the rest of their long journey.

∿

At nearly the same moment as Girlando said good-bye to his cousin in a flurry of embraces and kisses, Lieutenant Puglisi was in the sitting room of Mazzaglia's house.

"Is Don Pippino in?"

"Yes, but he's in bed. He doesn't feel so good. I'll go and ask if he can see you."

The maid walked away. And again the same fatigue of the body and heart that went into hiding whenever he was saying or doing something but which always emerged when he was alone, even if only for a moment, came over Puglisi. Realizing he couldn't stand on his own two feet, he leaned on the back of a chair and even thought he saw something dark flutter before his eyes. The maid returned.

"You can come in. Don Pippino's feeling better."

He followed her into Mazzaglia's bedroom. Don Pippino was sitting up in bed with three pillows behind his back. He was sallow, and his mouth hanging open as if short of breath. With a trembling hand he gestured to the policeman to sit down in an armchair beside the bed.

"I haven't got the breath to speak," said Don Pippino.

"I can see that. So, if you'll allow me, I'll ask you only one question."

Mazzaglia nodded yes, he could go ahead.

"Where's the Roman?"

And as Mazzaglia had raised his hand as if to make him stop, Puglisi continued, not allowing him time to catch his breath.

"I know that the Roman isn't here with you, since you would never welcome into your home someone capable of setting fire to a theatre and killing two innocent people without a second thought. You're not that kind of person. That's why I'm here to ask you: Where is this murderer hiding?"

"I don't know," said Don Pippino in a faint voice.

"But *I* know something: that you fell ill because you had something to do with this scoundrel."

Don Pippino squeezed his eyes shut and turned even paler.

"Please don't speak; I'll speak for you," Puglisi continued. "I've been racking my brains over this. So: I know you wouldn't associate with a scumbag like Traquandi, nor would Don Ninì Prestìa, who's an honorable man like yourself. And, I would bet my last lira Bellofiore wanted nothing to do with him, either. So, of all you Mazzinians, that leaves only one name. Decu. Am I wrong?"

Mazzaglia didn't say yes and he didn't say no.

"So it's Decu who's got the Roman in his house?"

The old man didn't budge.

"Thanks," said Puglisi, standing up. "I'm going to get him."

Don Pippino's hand shot out and gripped the policeman's arm tightly.

"Be careful. That Roman's a bad one."

Giagia my dear

Giagia my dear,

On this day, my beloved, I wish to reveal another of my secrets to you. So many have I entrusted to your heart's possession over the years of this our common path in life, Giagia, that they now hang like rare pearls in a necklace round your ivory neck. And since I see myself entirely reflected in them, it is as though I were forever blissfully close to your tenderest, most desirable flesh.

And now I wish to add a new pearl to the string.

Beloved Giagia, the question everyone is asking in Montelusa and the surrounding towns, particularly Vigàta, is this: What could be the reason why your husband, the Prefect, that is, the Solemn Representative of the State in these most ungracious parts, so obdurately wishes that the new theatre of Vigàta should be inaugurated with The Brewer of Preston, the opera by Luigi Ricci?

Spiteful tongues, who are by far the most numerous, having learned of the blood relation linking me to the impresario of said opera, have gauged my intentions by the measure of their own wretched hearts and most ignobly set about speculating on the presumed pecuniary interest I might have in exploiting such a blood tie. Whereas you know best of all how my family, and I myself first and foremost, have wished to sever relations with this person, ever since he showed himself to be not only an inveterate gambler and squanderer of fortunes, but also given to frequenting such women of ill repute as dancers, actresses, and singers.

And so? What was, then, the reason for the distinguished

Prefect's obstinate insistence? This is the question being asked in Montelusa and environs.

How hard I struggled, my darling, to have that opera performed in Vigàta! To attain my goal I had to face dark days and heated arguments with a serene spirit and undaunted courage. Yet you knew nothing of these tortured vicissitudes, darling Giagia, for I wished to spare you the lot of it by keeping it all secret from you, that you might suffer not at all if not for my occasional bouts of ill humor, for which I shall never cease to beg your forgiveness.

Yet before revealing the secret reason for my meddling in a decision that should have concerned solely, and freely, those appointed to manage the new Theatre of Vigàta, I must of necessity take a step back.

What sort of life was I leading in Florence in eighteen hundred and forty-seven? I was a young lawyer, from an upstanding, respected family, and yet an unspoken, morose agitation was corroding my soul. I wanted no part of any undertaking, considering them all empty and vain, and saw no other point to life than life's very ending, death, the final terminus. I cared not even for the amusements proper to youth, as I shut myself up in the sullen mutism of impassioned solitude. I belonged, Giagia, to that "vast graveyard of the drowned" of which Aleardi sang—Aleardi, the poet over whose pages, in the years that followed, we were to weep so many tears, heave so many sighs. But then came the evening, auspicious, unforgettable, when a fervent friend, the confidant of my discontent—Pepoli, remember?— dragged me from my lethal indolence and brought me to the Teatro della Pergola, where, for the first time in Florence, none other than The Brewer of Preston *was being performed, a work I had never heard mentioned before. It was with scarce enthusiam, needless to say, that I went with him.*

I had neither the heart nor the mind, my darling, to keep feigning a nonexistent and thus all the more evanescent interest in hearing those sounds and seeing those figures moving and singing onstage. Thus I decided that I should head back home at the end of the first act, duly excusing myself to my friend Pepoli. And it was precisely as I was on my way to the exit, stepping wearily through the festive crowd, that I first set eyes on you, my beloved. You were dressed all in blue like the heavens and were celestial indeed, as though your feet touched not the ground. I was as though struck by lightning, and I turned to stone. It lasted an instant, and then your eyes met mine. O God! In that instant my life was changed, turned upside down as by a beneficent earthquake, and what had earlier appeared to me gray and wan miraculously brightened and shone with vivid colors. To say it again with Aleardi, "Love spread the fertile wing" of everything. And you well know, Giagia, that as of that moment, I became eternally bound to you, with new strength and renewed purpose, considering life as . . .

～～

On his very skin, in the hair curling on his arms, Don Memè sensed that there was something suspicious in the way the town of Vigàta was getting ready for the inauguration of the theatre. But there was nothing to be done, for it wasn't anything concrete that gave him this feeling, but merely hints, silences, fleeting glances, brief smirks in the corners of people's mouths. Whereas he had pledged, in his person and on his honor, that all would go smoothly. But if things were to take a bad turn, how would he ever be able to face the prefect? And so he paced up and down the high street of Vigàta, looking askance at anyone who didn't appeal to him and noisily greeting anyone who happened to be in agreement with what he, first, and the prefect, second, wanted.

∿

. . . I retraced my steps not to listen to the opera through to the end, but so as not to subject my eyes to the desperate sorrow of not seeing you again. Heaven in its benevolence had seen to it that my orchestra seat was somewhat towards the back, so that the second-row box in which you sat with your loved ones was situated slightly ahead of me. Perhaps feeling the nape of your neck burning from my ardent gaze, at a certain point you slowly, haughtily turned . . . your eyes met mine . . . and at once I felt transformed—please don't laugh, my darling Giagia—into a soap bubble that began to float ever so lightly in air, flying up and out of the theatre, over the piazza, rising up until it could see the whole city diminished below . . .

∿

Arelio Butera and Cocò Cannizzaro had left Palermo early in the morning, at about four o'clock. Brokers of fava beans and grains, they were supposed to make an extensive business tour of the Montelusa province, going from town to town over the course of three days. While passing the time before they were supposed to meet with a wholesaler from Vigàta, they started walking down the main street of the town. In the course of their walk, they found themselves in front of a printed bill at either side of which stood, as if on guard, a man with a beret and a rifle on his shoulder.

They stopped to read what was written on the bill. Or, more precisely, Cocò started reading aloud, since reading and writing really weren't his friend Arelio's strong suits.

"'Special announcement,'" Cannizzaro read, "'for the evening of Wednesday, December twelfth. Gala inauguration of the new Teatro Re d'Italia of Vigàta. Sole performance of the immortal opera *The Brewer of Preston*, by Neapolitan maestro Luigi Ricci. Who has enjoyed many triumphs not only in Italy but also Worldwide. His many operas, from *The Thwarted Supper* to *The Sleepwalker*, have won the applause of Kings and Emperors, as well as that of the broader cultured public. Guaranteeing inevitable success in Vigàta are tenor Liborio Strano and soprano Maddalena Paolazzi, who will interpret the roles of the enamored brewer and his beautiful fiancée, Effy, respectively. Embellished with colorful décors and magnificent costumes, the performance will begin at six o'clock sharp in the evening. With best wishes to the public, all the singers, the orchestra with its fourteen professors of music under the direction of the Distinguished Maestro Eusebio Capezzato, and the Chorus of the Vocal Academy of Naples, await with hearts aflutter the applause of Vigàta's intelligent opera lovers, who shall kindly converge on the new Teatro Re d'Italia on the appointed date.'"

"I din't unnastand a bleedin' thing," said Arelio. "Whassit mean?"

"It means that tonight the new theatre opens and they're gonna show an opra about somebody that makes beer."

"You like beer, Cocò?"

"No."

"How come?"

"'Cause it makes me burp and piss."

"An' it makes *me* burp and piss and fart."

They laughed. But their laughter was interrupted by a polite voice.

"May I? Mind letting me in on the joke, so I can laugh, too?"

The two men turned around, surprised. The blue eyes,

broad, cordial smile, and sedate attitude of the man made them fall into the trap.

"Iss our business what we's laughin about. If you got somethin to laugh about too, then go ahead 'n' laugh," Cocò replied, grabbing Arelio's arm to get him to move along.

"Stop," said one of the two men in berets, taking the rifle off his shoulder. The two bean brokers stopped. With a violent gesture, Don Memè separated the two outsiders from behind and placed himself between them.

"I said I want to laugh, too."

Instinctively, Arelio raised a hand to strike him. Don Memè grabbed it in midflight and twisted it behind the man's back as he dealt a kick straight to the groin of Cocò, who fell to the ground whimpering and cupping his hands over his balls. Ten or so idlers and passersby stopped to look, keeping a proper distance.

Arelio was quick to recover, however, and took a step back, extracting a jackknife with a foot-long blade from his belt.

"Nah-ah-ah," said Don Memè in warning, right hand reaching into the rear pocket of his trousers where he kept his revolver. From the abrupt change in the man's face, Arelio realized that it wasn't worth the trouble, that the man wasn't making that gesture just for show. Arelio folded his jackknife and put it back in his belt.

"Sorry, sir," he said in a low voice.

"We all make mistakes," said Don Memè. "Have a good day."

He turned his back to the two men and walked away. He was pleased and felt like singing. Everyone had seen what would happen if they were to make fun of the opera. And indeed the whole town would be informed of this fact in less than an hour.

Arelio, meanwhile, was helping Cocò back on his feet, since he couldn't manage on his own, doubled over and moaning as he was. None of the people looking on made any sign of wanting to help.

"But where the hell did we make a mistake?" Arelio asked himself aloud.

He had no answer; nor did the idlers around him, who resumed idling, nor the passersby, who passed on by.

〜

. . . that was why I so obstinately wanted this opera to be performed in Vigàta. There is no other reason. And whatever the reason, no one shall ever discover it, for it shall remain sealed in the innermost recesses of your heart and mine. This evening we shall sit, one beside the other, in the royal box of the new theatre, no longer far from each other as before, and I shall squeeze your hand tightly. I shall squeeze it to remind you of the best moments of our first encounter. Let us enjoy together, my darling, this gift that time and chance have allowed me to offer you as a token of future happiness. With this I send you a kiss, sweet as you like it,

Yours for life,

Dindino

〜

He took an envelope, wrote "*To my Giagia*" on it, and, without sealing it, put it in his jacket pocket. At dinnertime he went into the bedroom and placed it visibly under the mirror of her dressing table. He did not, as hoped, receive a prompt reply, which led him to think that Giagia had perhaps not noticed it. Yet when he went back to the dressing table to look, the envelope was gone.

~~~

Giagia's silence continued during their ride in the carriage from Montelusa to Vigàta. The lady seemed distracted. One moment she was adjusting her hair, the next she was re-arranging her dress. Was it possible she had taken the letter and not read it? The prefect could not resist asking.

"Did you read my letter, Giagia?"

"Of hourse. Thank you, Dindino."

That was simply the way Giagia was. There was nothing to be done about it. A year after they had married, he gave her a pendant that he had had to sell two of his late grandfa-ther's farms to buy. And all she had said by way of reply was:

"Hute."

After a pause, as they were being tossed about by the treacherous road surface, she opened her mouth again and said:

"But you *are* mistahen, Dindino."

"Mistahen about what?"

"The date, Dindino. I certainly never attended the per-formance of this *Brewer*. I've never seen it at all. Never even heard of it."

"Are you johing?"

Before answering, she touched her hair, breast, left hip, right hip, eyes, and lips.

"No, dear Dindino, I'm not johing. I never went to the theatre that evening. I stayed at home with my granny. I had things of my own to do, and I felt very bad. I'm huite certain of it, Dindino. I even went and checked my diary. I stayed at home that night."

"But didn't we see each other for the first time at the Teatro della Pergola?"

"Of hourse we did, Dindino, but it was six days later. There wasn't this *Brewer* playing, but an opera by Bohherini. I think it was halled *La Giovannina* or something similar."

"It was called *La Clementina*. Now I remember," Bortuzzi said glumly, falling silent.

The oranges were more plentiful

The oranges were more plentiful than usual that year, Puglisi noticed as he and Catalanotti positioned themselves behind a low wall a few yards from Decu's house. The dawn arrived in the company of a cold, bothersome wind, and the day promised darkness. The lieutenant suffered the cold twofold, owing to lack of sleep. He had decided not to go to bed that night, certain that the moment he lay down he would have plunged into a leaden sleep lasting at least forty-eight hours. And so, after speaking with Don Pippino Mazzaglia the previous evening, he had gone home, washed himself, changed clothes, and started pacing about his room. After a while of this, he had felt the need to go outside and get some air, and so he'd headed to the beach and started walking along the water's edge, thinking of the folly he'd committed with Agatina. Folly because, were he to continue the liaison, as he desired, without fail her husband would find out. And, jealous as he was, he would revolt. While he, Puglisi, chief detective of police, a man of the law, would become the scandal of the town. He would be setting a bad example. Thus, no. With Agatina, the next time he saw her, everything had to appear as if nothing had ever happened between them, but not only that: Agatina herself had to understand that there would be no further encounters.

"If I stand here another five minutes without moving, I'll be stiff as a stockfish," Catalanotti said to him in a low voice, rubbing his fingers together to keep them from going numb.

"Don't you move from here," Puglisi said to him. "Cover me from behind and don't come out into the open until I call you."

The house of the Garzìa family, who had once been rich, prominent people, had long been going to ruin. The roof was half caved in, and the attic provided only partial shelter from the wind and rain because at several points it, too, was punctured, while the windows and the central French door on the main floor lacked panes and shutters. The upstairs rooms were clearly uninhabitable, and therefore Decu and his Roman friend must necessarily be sleeping on the ground floor. Hunched entirely forward, Puglisi dashed to the door. Nothing happened. Then he stepped to the side, extended an arm, and knocked. Nobody answered. He knocked harder.

"Whoozat?" asked a sleepy-sounding voice inside.

Puglisi became immediately convinced that the person who had answered was playacting. He was obviously pretending to have just woken up at that moment.

"It's me, Lieutenant Puglisi. I need to talk to you. Come outside."

"I'll be right there, just be patient a minute," said the voice, no longer sleepy but alert and attentive.

The door opened and Decu popped out in woolen underpants and jersey, a blanket draped over his shoulders.

"Good morning, Lieutenant. What is it?"

"Where's the Roman?"

Decu batted his eyelashes to display surprise, but he was not a good actor.

"What Roman?"

"The Roman who's here with you."

"Are you joking? I'm alone. Come inside and have a look for yourself."

"You go in first," ordered Puglisi, revolver in hand.

The search for the Roman lasted only a few minutes. There was no trace of the man. Puglisi began to feel prey to a blind rage. Someone had clearly been thinking ahead of him and had set things right by letting the Roman escape. But the game was not yet lost.

"Get dressed," he said to Decu. "We're going down to the station to have a little talk, you and me, alone, face-to-face. Then we'll see which of us is more clever."

Without saying a word, Decu sat down on the bed and bent forward to get his shoes. He was ready to do everything his cousin had advised. After all, there wasn't a bleeding shred of proof. Yet as he was feeling around under the bed for the shoe, his fingers felt the cold steel of the pistol he had hidden there the day before and forgotten about. Without his brain entering into the matter, he grabbed the gun by pure instinct and fired.

Hit square in the chest, Puglisi crashed against the wall, dropping his weapon, then slid down in a sitting position.

On the floor he moved as if to lie down, as if he wanted to get more comfortable.

At the sound of the gunshot, Catalanotti stood up from behind the wall and started running towards the house, cursing. He burst in, breathless, and saw Puglisi on the floor with a great big bloodstain over his chest, eyes closed. In front of him stood Decu, trembling and wan, the revolver having fallen from his hand.

"*Madonna santa!*" Catalanotti whispered, realizing all too well from experience that his friend and superior had died on the spot, snuffed out like a candle.

"I didn't mean to do it," Decu whined in a faint voice. "I didn't want to kill him. I couldn't help it."

Catalanotti stared at him. A creature, blondish, disgusting, with little hair, a sort of worm in the form of a man. And he was peeing his underpants, which began to drip.

"You couldn't help it?"

"No. I swear."

"I can't help it either," said Catalanotti, and he shot him in the face. Then he crouched next to Puglisi, took his head in his hands, kissed him on the forehead, and started to cry.

‹‹‹

The sky was beginning to lighten over by Serradifalco. They were crossing a deep valley fragrant with an overwhelming scent of oranges. Laurentano the bumpkin stopped.

"I need to pee," he said.

"Yeah, I gotta go too," concurred Traquandi. It had been six hours since they'd exchanged any words. They dismounted. The Roman went up to a tree, unbuttoned his fly, and started relieving himself. Right in front of him was an orange, hanging from a low branch. It was a thing of beauty, and he couldn't resist.

Holding his dick in his left hand, Traquandi raised his right hand to pick the fruit. And at that exact moment Laurentano shot him at the base of the skull. The Roman lurched forward, hitting his head against the tree trunk before falling facedown. Following the orders given him, Laurentano pulled out Traquandi's wallet, put the money that was inside (and there was a lot) into his own pocket, then made a little pile with the wallet, the outsider's suitcase, and everything that had been inside it. He set fire to the lot and waited with saintly patience for it all to burn, until only ashes remained. Then he attached the reins of the horse the Roman had ridden to his own saddle and headed back to Montelusa, or, more precisely, to the commissariat of Montelusa, where he served, each day, at the command of Dr. Meli.

⁓

That morning Don Memè, having plucked up his courage, appeared in the anteroom to the prefect's office.

"Please tell His Excellency I'm here," he said to Orlando.

The bailiff eyed him for a moment, then looked down and answered in a soft voice that was almost inaudible.

"His Excellency is very busy."

"Even for me?"

"For everyone, Don Memè. He told me expressly: I am busy for everyone, even the Eternal Father."

"And when can I come back?"

"I couldn't say."

Don Memè decided that it was undignified on his part to keep haggling with Orlando, who seemed to be taking pleasure in denying him. He turned around and made as if to leave, showing his usual smiling face to all present, but he was stopped by the bailiff's voice.

"Ah, Don Memè, I almost forgot. Dr. Vasconcellos would like to have a word with you. Please come with me."

They headed down a long corridor, Orlando in front and Don Memè behind. Vasconcellos was the chief of the prefect's cabinet, a sort of midget known as *u sacchiteddru,* "the little sack," either because of his diminutive stature or his habit of wearing clothes that made him lose all semblance of human form. Some who knew him well called him *u sacchiteddru di vipere*.

Arriving in front of a door, Orlando signaled to Don Memè to wait, then knocked and went in. A moment later he came back out.

"He's waiting for you."

The chief of the cabinet, who, until two days earlier would have doubled over bowing in reverence to Don Memè, not only did not answer his greeting, but did not even rise from his chair, which sat on a raised platform to receive him. If there were any need for it, thought Don Memè, this was the proof that a new wind was changing the course of every boat on the water.

"His Excellency," said Vasconcellos, "left this parcel for you. It contains books. He said you should return them to their legitimate owner and thank him for the loan."

Surely it was *The Archaelogical History of Sicily*, the one he had forced the notary Scimè to give him so that he could make a gift of it in turn to the prefect. As he was picking up the parcel, Vasconcellos stared at him with beady eyes that looked truly snakelike and hissed:

"Have a pleasant Lent, Signor Ferraguto."

Don Memè, distracted, fell into the trap like a stewed pear.

"Lent? In December?"

"December or January, the Carnival is over."

The sourpuss had done it. Vasconcellos had succeeded in shooting his squid ink, his viperlike venom.

~~~

The rage he felt was so great that, as he rode home in his little carriage, Don Memè's head was abuzz as if full of flies, wasps, bees, and bumblebees. And since rage in the end always gives bad counsel, Don Memè decided to turn the horse around and go to a small, secluded house of his near Sanleone. Upon arriving, he halfheartedly ate a little tumazzo cheese and some hard bread soaked in wine. Then he noticed that the twenty-odd orange trees he had in his garden were so laden with fruit that the branches were bending. So he took a wicker basket and set to work on the first tree in the grove. He didn't want to think. He would decide what needed to be done after a good night's sleep. But one thing was as certain as the sun: the prefect was showing himself to be a bigger jackass than he had realized, if he thought he could get rid of Don Memè so easily. He would make him pay, and pay dearly, for the affront he had made him suffer at the prefecture before the eyes of everyone.

When the basket was full, he emptied it into a big chest made of reeds and then went to work on the second tree. He toiled for three hours without even realizing it. He was almost done when he heard the sound of a horse approaching. Glancing towards the gate, he saw that it was Gaetanino Sparma, the so-called field watcher of the Honorable Deputy Fiannaca. Don Memè went out to meet him, as was only proper.

"What a sight for sore eyes! A magnificent surprise! How did you know I'd come out here?"

"When I get it into my head to find someone, I find him, even if he's turned himself into a flea on a dog's rump."

They laughed. Sparma dismounted, came into the house, and accepted a glass of wine. After waiting the proper amount of time so that the question wouldn't seem instrusive or fearful, Don Memè asked: "To what do I owe the honor?"

"The Honorable Deputy sent me. He'd like to talk to you."

"Today?"

"No, no, at your leisure. It's nothing important."

"And how is the Honorable Deputy? Well?"

"With thanks to the Lord, he's in good health. But this morning he got very angry."

"With whom, if I may ask?"

"Somebody from Favara. The Honorable Fiannaca said this man from Favara didn't understand the difference between a common bully and a man of honor."

"Oh, yes? And what did the Honorable Deputy say the difference was?"

"I'll tell you in a minute," said Sparma, "but I don't want to bother you with idle chatter. Just keep doing what you were doing. Actually, if you like, I can give you a hand picking the oranges, which are truly spectacular."

"Thanks," said Don Memè, on his guard. The other man's speech seemed suspicious to him; he wanted to find out what he was driving at.

They went out of the house, and Gaetanino grabbed a basket and started picking oranges from the same tree as Don Memè.

"The difference," said the field watcher, "lies not only in appearance, but also in substance. For whatever reason, this gentleman from Favara had teamed up with the chief of police. They became hand in glove with each other. And so he started doing himself, on the police chief's behalf, things that the police—that is, the law—can't do on its own. Abuses of power, iniquities, shameful things. Pummeling a man in public, sending an innocent to jail . . . These sorts of things, says the Honorable Deputy, concern appearance. But in order not to lose face, and especially not to let the friends who place their trust in you lose face, you need substance. If it comes out, however, that you've got no substance, that you're empty inside, then you're just a branch in the wind. You become an overbearing servant and, what's worse, an overbearing servant of the law, which is a crooked thing by nature. Do you agree, sir?"

"Of course I agree."

"Now a bully who takes himself for a man of honor can do damage, a lot of damage." He paused and wiped his sweaty forehead with his sleeve. "My lord, how much I've been talking! And perhaps I haven't even made myself clear!"

"You've made yourself very clear. Couldn't be any clearer," Don Memè said darkly.

This, then, was the jist of the argument: he should submit himself to judgment, explain his relationship with the prefect, and justify himself. He burned with resentment at the insult of having been called a bully. He no longer wanted Sparma in his hair.

"The baskets are full," he said. "Let's go unload them."

He bent down to pick up his basket. And it was the last act of his life, because Gaetanino, convinced he had given him enough reasons to fulfill his obligation, opened his straight razor, grabbed Don Memè by the hair, yanked his head back, and slit his throat, at the same time taking a leap backwards to avoid getting spattered with blood. The field watcher was a master at handling the razor, even though he had never been a barber in his life. Then, with the tip of his boot, he turned the dead man belly-up and stuck a sheet of blank letterhead paper between his teeth. The letterhead read: ROYAL PREFECTURE OF MONTELUSA. That way, whoever wanted to understand would understand.

Chapter I

O thers might have written a book of fantasy, a novel, about the events that occurred in Vigàta on the evening of December 10, 1874, when the Teatro Re d'Italia, just inaugurated, was destroyed by flames a few hours after the gala opening performance. Certainly a novelist would have found more than a few opportunities to stoke his lively imagination, since many points of the story appeared obscure from the start and, precisely because they were never clarified, left the field wide open to the wildest, most delirious sorts of speculation.

I, however, feel practically duty bound not to yield to the lures of the imagination, precisely because I myself, not quite ten years old at the time, was the first to sound the alarm in Montelusa, alerting my late father, a mining engineer who died some years ago, to the great fire. With an indomitable sense of altruism and generosity of intent, my good father gathered together some of his collaborators and raced to Vigàta with a device of his own conception and construction, designed to extinguish fires or at least to contain them. And I must declare, with filial pride, that his clever use of this machine spared the already stricken town of Vigàta even further destruction.

It is therefore my intention, some forty and more years after the event, to keep within the bounds of a straightforward testimony, and to organize the story in accordance with a reconstruction based solidly on the facts as they emerge from the documents of the investigation, letters, and testimonies.

I should begin by saying that at the time, Vigàta, at once a fishing and farming town, had a population of some seven thousand souls and was territorially part of the province of Montelusa, even though it was geographically much closer to another provincial capital, Girgenti. A chronicler of the time, Professor Baldassare Corallo, wrote:

> With the gradual improvement of economic conditions, our town began to move towards the sort of civilized prosperity that characterized Italian life in general. Even the middle class aimed at raising the cultural level and began to welcome the premises of civilization enthusiastically.

One of these premises, apparently, was the construction of a theatre that would be not only a place of amusement, however lofty, but also an ideal meeting place, a sort of assembly hall where the community could gather from time to time either to hear the sublime creations of visiting artists or to debate matters specific to the town itself.

The proposal for the projected theatre, unanimously approved in a vote of the Muncipal Council on March 27, 1870, led, after private negotiations, to the signing of a contract with the firm Tempore Novo of Misilmesi. Almost immediately, insinuating and malicious rumors began to spread among the local population, saying that the head of this contracting firm, while never officially avowed, was none other than the Honorable Fiannaca, deputy of the Chamber, to whose same political party the mayor of Vigàta, the *ragioniere* Casimir Pulitanò, also belonged.

Nothing more slanderous and mendacious could have been imagined about Deputy Fiannaca, whose political career was a mirror of his unimpeachably upstanding comportment in all walks of life. He was elected with overwhelming public consensus to no less than two terms of legislative office and even filled, in the most dignified fashion, the position of Undersecretary to the Ministry of the Interior, which is saying a great deal.

An anarchist, one Federico Passerino, saw fit to publish a scurrilous, ignoble broadside against the Honorable Fiannaca, in which he asserted, among other things, a hypothetical alliance between the deputy and Mayor Pulitanò concerning the abovementioned contract. It should be immediately pointed out that Passerino, a man who serves no God, Country, or Family, who has no place or role in society and lacks the qualities that allow a man to participate in civilized humankind, was once personally and publicly saved by the Honorable Fiannaca when he was understandably assailed by a number of the politician's supporters indignant at the multiple insinuations this despicable individual spewed at the hardworking deputy at every available opportunity. More to pacify the people's spirits than for any desire for personal satisfaction, the deputy decided to take the high road of Justice, drafting a formal complaint against Passerino, supported by an abundance of evidence. And indeed the latter was found guilty of defamation by the Court of Montelusa. It should

also be added, for the sake of historical thoroughness, that
Passerino, his wife Margherita, and their young son Andrea,
known as Nirìa, all met horrible deaths when a bomb the
anarchist was assembling at his home exploded. On this
occasion as well, a few malicious rumors claimed that in reality the bomb had been thrown through an open window
into Passerino's home. But I mention these rumors only out
of concern for impartiality. In that family's tragedy, most
people recognized the hand of God.

The contractors, in any case, abided by the agreement,
with, however, a few cost increases owing to the fall in the
value of the lira, and the theatre was ready for inauguration a
mere ten months after the completion date envisaged in the
contract awarded.

Many and varied, and quite fantastical, were instead the
rumors that swirled in the province over the opera chosen for
the inauguration. At that time the province of Montelusa was
governed by two outstanding representatives of the state.
The first was His Excellency the Prefect, Cavalier Eugenio
Bortuzzi, a Florentine; the second was the commissioner of
police, Cavalier Everardo Colombo, a Milanese.

Upon first arriving on our island, Mr. Bortuzzi immediately took great care, as was his duty, to acquaint himself
personally with the people and affairs of our province, which
he would be called upon to govern righteously, as indeed he
did. By the direct testimony of Carmelo Ferraguto, at that
time the fifteen-year-old son of the late Emanuele Ferraguto—
known familarly to all as *u zu Memè*, "Uncle Memè," for the
promptness with which he was always ready, whatever the
circumstance, to meet the needs of his fellow locals, whatever they might be—I learned how His Excellency the

Prefect was able to use Mr. Ferraguto's father, whom he knew well, to acquire a most thorough knowledge of local matters, that he might have the most exhaustive possible picture of the conditions in which the province was living.

Unfortunately, Emanuele Ferraguto's commendable work was cut short when he was barbarously murdered by unknown assassins for equally unknown reasons, as he was unsuspectingly setting about harvesting the oranges in a small grove of his.

A man of deep culture and highly refined intellect (nor could he be otherwise, having been born in Florence, the supreme birthplace of Art), Prefect Bortuzzi felt an obligation to educate the people of Vigàta in matters of Art, indeed to accompany them, like a father, in their first steps towards the Sublime.

As a private citizen—and not as representative of the authority invested in him—Mr. Bortuzzi, during the course of a luncheon at the home of a friend, expressed to the Marchese Antonino Pio di Condò, president of the Administrative Council of the theatre, the humble opinion that an opera such as *The Brewer of Preston*, by Maestro Luigi Ricci, might well serve as the first of an ideal *gradus ad Parnassum* for the people of Vigàta. This idea—presented, I repeat, with the sole intent of avoiding a sense of dismay in a population certainly not yet ready to appreciate in full the beauty and depth of operas subtler in theme and more complex in composition— gave rise to a dangerous misunderstanding. A few members of the council saw—indeed chose to see—His Excellency's gracious suggestion as an imposition of authority, something in fact quite foreign to the prefect's moral character. As a result of the heated diatribes that ensued, the Marchese Antonino Pio di Condò found himself forced to turn in his resignation. And after troubled discussions and enflamed polemics, Commendator Massimo Però was elected in his place. However, upon the justified advice of one member of the council, Professor Amilcare Ragona (who had actually gone to Naples for the express purpose of seeing a performance of the opera in question), Commendator Però resubmitted *The Brewer of Preston* as the opera for the inauguration.

What to say, other than that at this point the resistence of one part of the council increased, the insinuations multiplied, and the most malicious of rumors began to circulate without any restraint whatsoever? So great indeed was the spate of slander that His Excellency Bortuzzi was forced, however reluctantly, to dissolve the Administrative Council and appoint an extraordinary commissar in the person of Sisinio Trincanato, a high functionary of the prefecture whose gift for impartiality was indisputable. And yet on this occasion, too, another wicked rumor spread, namely that Mr. Trincanato, being the brother-in-law of Mr. Emanuele Ferraguto, would never be able to avoid the combined pressures of the prefect and Ferraguto himself. Whereas, as could have been expected, Mr. Trincanato yet again gave proof of his absolute independence of judgment. Indeed, he did even more: before making his decision, he listened to the opinions of several members of the dissolved council and consulted eminent citizens of Vigàta, and only after having done so did he democratically draw his conclusions. And in this manner the definitive choice of *The Brewer of Preston* was made.

Contrary to what was written and said in newspapers and social clubs unfavorable to the governing party, the performance of the opera was not disturbed by any significant expressions of dissent. There were exclamations of wonderment at the beauty of the stage décors and the opulence of the costumes, not to mention at the excellence of the music and the skill of the singers. Some uncivilized behavior was demonstrated by a number of spectators seated in the gallery, but this involved above all naïve commentaries made by people who had never set foot in a theatre before and were unaware of the proper etiquette required in such a setting. These undisciplined spectators should have been called back to more civilized behavior by the Superintendent of the Public Order, Police Lieutenant Sebastiano Puglisi. But this is the sore point of the whole unfortunate affair, and I shall attempt to place it in the proper light. Mr. Puglisi was by nature a vulgar man of violent temperament, attributes aggravated by an adulterous affair he was carrying on with a young Vigàta woman whose sister, a widow, met a horrendous death as a result of the theatre fire. Possibly to maintain the unfaithful woman with lavish sums of money, Mr. Puglisi had lent his services to protecting the clandestine numbers circuit, a scourge across Sicily which in those days prospered thanks to the hidden screen provided by the very people who should have prosecuted and halted such illegal activities. The repressive actions promptly taken by the prefect and police commissioner brought to light Puglisi's involvement in this shady traffic. Still, Puglisi—nobody knows how—escaped by the skin of his teeth. And thanks to an error of judgment on the part of the commissioner, an error owing to his innate generosity of spirit, the lieutenant was able to remain at his post and continue to weave his schemes. Thus during the opera performance, he, as is customary with all wicked spirits, instead of intervening to dissuade, placate, or win people over, let himself fall into a sort of haughty indifference.

It should be said, for the sake of documentation, that two

days after the theatre fire, Puglisi died ignominiously. As was later established, he had gone to a meeting between mafiosi, fugitives, and brigands at the house of a certain Diego Garzìa, a young man from a once eminent, now impoverished family, who had gone astray perhaps because of his family's misfortunes. That the gathering was convened to decide upon further criminal undertakings is beyond the shadow of a doubt. Indeed Puglisi attended the meeting armed with his personal revolver (his regulation firearm was found in the drawer of his office desk in Vigàta). And, in any case, if his presence there was part of an operation aimed at thwarting future actions of the criminal underworld, he would have been obliged first to alert the Commissariat of Police and then the men working under his command. But he informed nobody and went alone, a sign that he didn't want any witnesses. Some sort of argument must have broken out inside the Garzìa home, probably concerning the distribution of ill-gotten gains, a sort of settling of accounts, as they say, during which Garzìa and Puglisi grabbed their weapons and killed each other. The investigation promptly conducted by the new Detective Superintendent of Vigàta, Lieutenant Catalonotti, resoundingly confirmed this sequence of events.

There was also talk—quite out of place—of the intervention of a company of mounted militiamen during the events that led to the burning of the theatre, a company under the command of Captain Villaroel (who later ended his career as a colonel of the Royal Carabinieri). While it is true that a platoon of militiamen had drawn up in a line outside the theatre to protect the authorities gathered there, this formation was little more than an honor guard. About halfway through the second act, a number of drunken young hooligans began to scream and shout in the piazza in front of the theatre, for no other reason than to create a disturbance. This was why Captain Villaroel decided to inform the spectators that it was not advisable for people to leave the theatre alone or in small groups—specifically so they would not find themselves caught up in any unpleasant altercations. Apparently inexplicable, on the other hand, was the reaction of panic to the unexpected "clinker" (as they say in musical jargon) hit by the otherwise outstanding soprano Maddalena Paolazzi. As we know, a "clinker," or false note, is the sort of unfortunate accident than can occur in any theatre to even the most exceptional singers; yet never, in human memory, had this sort of mistake triggered, in any theatre in the world, such mad terror, which, indeed, cannot be defined otherwise. Through patient investigation and the help of preeminent scholars of the human mind, I have arrived at a rational explanation for this apparently irrational reaction, which I shall later set forth.

That leaves us to speak of the fire itself. It occurred, as has been established, at least two hours after the performance ended, when people had long returned in peace to their late-evening domestic concerns. The principal question is therefore the following: What caused such a violent fire to break out?

As the flames were still besieging the theatre, it became common belief that the disaster had been unintentionally triggered by a still-lighted cigar butt that had been carelessly dropped near something (like a curtain, armchair, or carpet) that might easily catch fire. And the two intervening hours appeared reasonably to be the perfect amount of time needed to pass between the dropping of the cigar, the slow process of combustion, and the outbreak of flames. Not content with this explanation, dictated by common sense, some wanted at all costs to insinuate another that lent itself better to the purposes of those who wanted to take advantage of the situation to call into question the actions of the established authorities. People spoke, for example, of the presence in town of a dangerous affiliate of the Mazzinian faction, and we must not, moreover, forget that at the time, republican tremors were running through the island, to the point that Mazzini himself was arrested a few months later while attempting a clandestine landing at Palermo. Be that as it may, no trace whatsoever was found of this mysterious revolutionary's passage through Vigàta, neither at the Royal Police Commissariat of Montelusa nor at the Constabulary of Vigàta. Officer Catalanotti, right-hand man of the notorious Puglisi, asserted for good measure that his superior had never so much as mentioned to him that he was aware of the presence in town of any violent agitator or presumed arsonist.

The book by the Honorable Paolino Fiannaca, titled *Sicilian Battles*, gives, moreover, generous credit to the republicans of Vigàta, who were nevertheless his political adversaries, and deems them above any suspicion of scurrility. The thesis of arson was, however, put forward (without anyone specific being assigned responsibility for the reprehensible act) by a young employee of the Property Insurers' Assocation, according to whom the fire had been started when two ceramic piggy banks filled with kerosene and made to explode with lighted fuses were thrown under the stage of the theatre. The utterly fanciful nature of this reconstruction was demonstrated shortly thereafter by Dr. Meli, who had taken over the investigation following the violent death of Lieutenant Puglisi, having been assigned the task by Commissioner Colombo.

Dr. Meli (who was to conclude his career in brilliant fashion by serving a high function at the Ministry of the Interior in Rome) irrefutably proved that those two piggy banks had belonged to the two young sons of the theatre's custodian, who, with typically childish mistrust, had hidden them under the stage. Ultimate confirmation was at last established when investigators found, near the shards of the piggy banks, a number of small coins earlier overlooked due to the damages caused by the fire.

Directly and indirectly, this fire caused the painful, excruciating loss of three human lives.

And here I am forced to look ahead to an episode upon which I should rather not have dwelt, both for the gravity of the matter and for the ignoble stench emanating from it. In brief: the flames emitted by the blaze reached a small three-story building standing directly behind the theatre. Two people in it died, a young widow and a man who, at first glance, appeared to have lost his life in a generous attempt to save her. This, at least, was what might be inferred from the positions of the two bodies. In reality, however, the whole thing was a macabre, indeed ignoble, scene staged by Lieutenant Puglisi. The young widow had died in her sleep, asphyxiated by smoke, like the man, who was her lover and with whom she had enjoyed illicit sexual congress until a few moments before. Suborned by his mistress, who was the widow's sister, Puglisi moved and manipulated the bodies in such a way as to make it seem as if the widow was alone in her bed and the man had tried to enter from the balcony to save her. Officer Catalanotti, however, became immediately aware of the obscene charade and, a few hours later, having fully established the facts confirming his correct hypothesis,

drafted a memorandum, a report to Dr. Meli that unequivocally reestablished the truth.

One who did, on the other hand, lose his life in a generous attempt to save the young widow was Dr. Salvatore
Gammacurta, one of Vigàta's two medical doctors. Realizing
that the flames were threatening the building behind the theatre, the doctor remembered that the widow, a patient of his,
lived on the top floor, and tried to save her by climbing up a
small mountain of salt that had been deposited almost directly
against the rear wall of the dwelling. His attempt was cut
short by a heart attack that struck him in the midst of his
heroic, altruistic act. The wounds found on his body can be
attributed, according to the autopsy conducted by the official
physician of the commissariat, to the countless obstacles
Gammacurta encountered in his ill-fated journey.

But we shall have ample opportunity to discuss this and
other as yet unknown episodes in the chapters that follow.

Author's Note

The *Report on the Social and Economic Conditions of Sicily (1875–1876)* (*Inchiesta sulle condizioni sociali ed economiche della Sicilia*)—not the similar study conducted by Franchetti and Sonnino, but the parliament's own inquest—was finally published in 1969 by Cappelli publishers in Florence and immediately proved to be a gold mine for me. From the report's questions, answers, observations, and quotations were born the novel *Hunting Season* (*La stagione della caccia*) and the essay *The Bull of Reconciliation* (*La bolla di componenda*).

The present novel increases my debt. In a hearing dated December 24, 1875, the researchers conducting the study listened to a journalist named Giovanni Mulè Bertòlo to learn about the attitude of the population of Caltanissetta towards the fledgling national government's policies. At a certain point, the journalist says that things immediately began to improve upon the departure of the local prefect, a Florentine by the name of Fortuzzi who had become particularly despised by the population. He said: "Fortuzzi wanted to study Sicily through the engravings in books. But if a book had no plates, that didn't matter . . . He was always shut up within four walls, with only three or four individuals around him, on whom he depended for advice."

The last straw came the day when Fortuzzi, who was supposed to inaugurate the new theatre of Caltanissetta, insisted that the opera to be performed should be *The Brewer of Preston*. "He even wanted to impose his music on us, the barbarians of this city! And by paying for it with our money!" Giovanni Mulè Bertòlo exclaimed in indignation. And Fortuzzi succeeded, despite the opposition of local authorities. The best part of all this is that it was never found out why the Florentine prefect was so adamant about the *Brewer*. Naturally, there were numerous incidents during the inaugural performance. Among other things, a postal employee who had noisily expressed his disapproval was transferred the following day ("He had to quit his job because he had an annual salary of only 700 lire and couldn't afford to leave Caltanissetta"), and the singers were overwhelmed by a booing, hissing audience.

Something even more serious must have happened, because the journalist says that, at a certain point, "mounted militiamen entered the theatre with armed troops." But the parliamentary commission chose to gloss over the rest and moved on to another subject.

This story, however scanty in detail in the report, caught my attention, and I began to develop it. The result is this novel, which is entirely invented, aside from the point of departure, of course.

I thank Dirk Karsten van den Berg for having got hold of the libretto and score for Luigi Ricci's *The Brewer of Preston*.

I dedicate this story to Alessandra, Arianna, and Francesco, who will read it when they grow up and, hopefully, will hear their grandfather's voice in it.

A. C. (1995)

P. S.

Having got this far in the book—that is, to the Author's Note at the end—what readers still remain will certainly have noticed by now that the chapter sequence I have presented here is merely a suggestion. Every reader is invited, if he or she so wishes, to establish his or her own personal order.

Notes

1 It was a frightful night, downright scary: A variation on the famous opening sentence of Edward Bulwer-Lytton's 1830 novel, *Paul Clifford*: "It was a dark and stormy night." According to Camilleri, however, his reference here is the book-length comic by Charles M. Schulz, *It Was a Dark and Stormy Night, Snoopy*. Schulz first used the quotation in a comic strip in 1965. The reader should note, moreover, that the opening sentence and title of each chapter of the present book either quotes the first line of a famous book or is a variation thereof. Each reference will be duly documented as the story progresses.

2 an acetylene lamp on some lost *paranza*: A *paranza* is a small fishing boat with a lateen sail and jib. The acetylene lamp is used to attract fish at night.

5 *zolfatari*: Sulphur miners.

9 A spectre is haunting the musicians of Europe: A play on the opening line of *The Communist Manifesto* (1848), by Karl Marx and Friedrich Engels: "A specter is haunting Europe: the specter of Communism."

14 "the swan of Busseto's": A reference to Giuseppe Verdi (1813–1901), who was raised in the north Italian town of Busseto.

14 *"Abietta zingara . . . Tacea la notte placida . . . Chi del gitano . . . Stride la vampa . . . Il balen del tuo sorriso . . . Di quella pira . . . Miserere":* The titles and first lines of famous arias from Verdi's *Il Trovatore* (1853).

15 *Una furtiva lacrima*: Aria from Gaetano Donizetti's *L'Elisir d'Amore* (1832).

15 *Una voce poco fa*: Aria from Gioacchino Rossini's *Barber of Seville* (1816).

17 *"Ah, non credea mirarti"*: Aria from act II, scene 2, of *La Sonnambula* (1831), by Vincenzo Bellini: *Ah!, non credea mirarti / si presto estinto o fior; / passasti al par d'amore, / che un giorno sol durò / . . . / Potria novel vigore / il pianto mio recarti, / ma ravvivar l'amore / il pianto mio, ah no, no non può.*

17 *"Qui la voce sua soave"*: Aria from act II of *I Puritani* (1835), by Vincenzo Bellini: *Qui la voce sua soave / Mi chiamava e poi sparì. / Qui giurava esser fedele . . .*

17 *"Vi ravviso, o luoghi ameni"*: Aria from act I of *La Sonnambula*, by Vincenzo Bellini: *Vi ravviso, o luoghi ameni, / in cui lieti, in cui sereni / sì tranquillo i dì passai della prima della prima gioventù . . .*

18 *"Suoni la tromba e intrepido"*: Aria from act II of *I Puritani*, by Vincenzo Bellini: *Suoni la tromba e intrepido / io pugnerò da forte: / bello è affrontar la morte / gridando libertà . . .*

19 Would he try to raise the mosquito net?: A slight variation on the opening line of *Man's Fate* (*La condition humaine*) by André Malraux (first published in 1933): "Should he try to raise the mosquito-netting?" (translation by Haakon M. Chevalier).

19 *pappataci*: *Phlebotomus papatasi*, an Old-World species of sand fly.

23 he brought the fingers of his right hand together, *a cacocciola*, **artichoke-like, and shook them up and down repeatedly:** This phrase describes the typically Italian hand gesture that is meant to ask a question. It can variously mean: *Why? What? Where? How?* and so on, or, more specifically, *What do you mean?* or *What's wrong with you?* or *What are you doing?* The gesture is used all around the Mediterrenean, by Spaniards, Arabs, Greeks, etc., but is most often associated with Italians, especially southern Italians. *Cacocciola* is Sicilian for "artichoke."

29 Get me Emanuele: An oblique reference to the opening to Melville's *Moby-Dick*: "Call me Ishmael." The reference is more recognizable in the original Italian text, since "get me" and "call me" both translate as "chiamami." Thus "Chiamami Ismaele," the start of the Italian translation of *Moby-Dick*, becomes "Chiamami Emanuele."

29 Cavalier *Dottor* Eugenio Bortuzzi: In Italy, the title of "doctor" or *dottore* is conferred upon anyone with a university degree. "Cavaliere" is an honorific title ("Knight") conferred on the bearer by the government.

31 *ragioniere* Ilio Ginnanneschi: *Ragioniere* is a title given those who complete a course of study (usually two years) in *ragioneria*, a sort of low-level accounting degree.

31 "Ah, how splendid our unified Italy is!": In the wake of the unification of Italy in 1870, government posts in the South were often filled by people from the Italian mainland: ". . . postmaster Ugo Bordin, from the Veneto, the *dottor* Carlo Alberto Pautasso, Esq., of Asti, director of the tax office, and the *ragioniere* Ilio Ginnanneschi, of Prato, an employee at the land registry." By having these same Northern Italians provide Don Memè with his alibi, Camilleri is wryly pointing to the *national* effort at corruption in the fledgling Italian state, for which Southerners alone are often scapegoated.

32 "They honfuse me": In accentuating the many cultural differences between the continental Italians and Sicilians in this book, and among the continental Italians themselves, Camilleri has included a great variety of divergences of speech, expressions, and dialect. In addition, to highlight Prefect Borduzzi's pompous Florentine manner, the author has translated orthographically the Tuscan habit of aspirating or sometimes suppressing the hard "c" (or "k") sound when it falls between vowels or at the beginning of a word. Thus when Bortuzzi says, for example, "We're at the gates with stones in our hands," the original Italian is written "*Siamo alle porte hoi sassi*," whereas it would normally be ". . . *coi sassi*." To give another example, a Tuscan will pronounce *la casa* as either *la hasa* or *la 'asa*. To carry over some of the humor and derision created in the original text by these strange orthographies, I have taken the liberty of making Prefect Bortuzzi aspirate almost all cases of hard "c" sounds that fall between vowels. Here, therefore, "confuse" becomes "honfuse." Perhaps the most absurd instance of this idiosyncrasy of speech in this book is when Giagia, the prefect's wife, pronounces the name of the Italian composer Boccherini as *Bohherini* (see p. 212).

33 "a *lupara* hidden in your trousers": *Lupara* ("wolf-gun") is the Sicilian term for sawn-off shotgun, formerly the weapon of preference of the Mafia.

34 "Punta Raisi's not a very good place for kites": And yet in the modern age it became the site of the airport of Palermo, despite the treacherous winds described in the short paragraph that follows this statement. Indeed, airplanes often encounter the same problems as the kites mentioned here, not to mention that the surrounding terrain is mountainous, making it the most dangerous airport in Europe. Rumor has it that the site was chosen to satisfy the desires of the Mafia.

37 On the morning of the day he was killed: An echo of the opening of *Chronicle of a Death Foretold*, by Gabriel García Márquez: "On the day they were going to kill him, Santiago Nasar got up at five-thirty in the morning . . ." (translated by Gregory Rabassa, Knopf, 1982).

39 *"Friends! To the brewery / we merrily run!"*: The libretto passages in Camilleri's text are taken directly from the 1847 original of Luigi Ricci's *Il Birraio di Preston*. I have translated them into English to facilitate comprehension of the audience's reactions to them.

43 "No need to look anywhere for horns. They grow all by themselves": In Italian, "to grow horns" is to be cuckolded.

43 *"with his unpleasant vocation / of living by the balls . . . of the cannon"*: In this instance I had to take a little liberty in the translation of the original libretto to create a line that would evoke the sort of derision that takes place in the theater. The original states *"Se quel brutto mestiero / di stare tra le palle e la mitraglia . . ."* Not missing an opportunity to make sport of some infelicitous phrasing, Camilleri has the audience burst into laughter after the phrase *"stare tra le palle . . . ,"* which is a rather vulgar way of saying "to be in the way" or, in a sense, "to be a pain in the ass." Literally, it means "to get between one's balls." In the libretto's context, however, *palle* is intended to mean "bullets" and the whole phrase to mean "that nasty job / of living between bullets and guns."

47 **"Ladies and, so to speak, gentlemen"**: The opening line recited by Nyukhin at the start of Anton Chekhov's *On the Harmful Effects of Tobacco* (1886, 1902).

57 **Turiddru Macca, son:** The opening of Giovanni Verga's "Cavalleria Rusticana" (1884), the short story, later turned into a play, that served as the basis of the opera of the same name by Pietro Mascagni, with a libretto by Giovanni Targioni-Tozzetti and Guido Menasci.

66 **Only the young have such feelings:** An echo of the opening of Joseph Conrad's novella *The Shadow-Line* (1917): "Only the young have such moments."

75 **"You know how I feel about this":** A direct quote of the opening line to Leonardo Sciascia's 1987 novel *Porte aperte* (*Open Doors*).

75 *Piemontese falso e cortese,* **as the saying went:** "Piedmontese are false and polite," an Italian commonplace that has fallen somewhat out of use in our time.

79 **From the moment Vidusso walked out, the prefect had been sitting with his head in his hands, sputtering curses that grew more and more elaborate as he invented them:** The Tuscans are known for improvising curses, to the point that some Tuscan villages even have summer contests to see who can come up with the most creative, blasphemous curse. Never having witnessed any such competitions myself, I was once told, however, that one year the winner of a certain village's contest had said: "*Madonna impestata*," a curse of manifold meanings, perhaps the most immediate being "Syphilitic Madonna."

85 The early morning sun hung milky and wan behind layers of cloud: An almost exact quote of the opening sentence of "Tonio Krüger," the story by Thomas Mann: "The early morning sun, poor ghost of itself, hung milky and wan behind layers of cloud . . ." (translated by H. T. Lowe-Porter. Thomas Mann, *Stories of Three Decades*. New York: Knopf, 1936).

93 Late as usual: The opening line of a short novel by Aldous Huxley, *After the Fireworks* (1930).

102 I wish either my father or my mother: The opening to chapter one of *Tristram Shandy* (1760), by Laurence Sterne.

105 the *Meo Patacca*: The *Meo Patacca*, by Giuseppe Berneri (1637–1701), whose full title is *Meo Patacca ovvero Roma in Festa nei trionfi di Vienna*, is a seriocomic "epic" written in Roman dialect. It remains an important document on the language, customs, and sensibilities of the Romans in the late seventeenth century.

110 By now everyone knew him as Don Ciccio: An almost exact echo of the opening line of *Quer pasticciaccio brutto de Via Merulana* (*That Awful Mess on Via Merulana*), by Carlo Emilio Gadda, which begins: "By now everyone called him Don Ciccio."

113 the Temple of Concordia: The Temple of Concordia is the most important and best preserved of the seven Greek temples, all in the Doric style, preserved in the Valley of Temples outside of Agrigento, Sicily, the city that serves as the model for Camilleri's fictional Montelusa.

113 *Dio bonino*: "Good little God." Another example of Tuscan creativity in cursing, in this case euphemistically. See note to page 79 on page 241.

114 *"Madonna 'amiciaia"*: "Shirt-making Madonna." Another instance of the Tuscan elision of the hard "c" between vowels. Normally the word would be *camiciaia*. See note to page 32 on page 239.

117 *"tanger . . . Étagère"*: In the Sicilian dialect of the region of Agrigento (where Camilleri sets his story), the word *tanger*, derived from the French *étagère*, is used for a variety of furnishings that range from sets of shelves to pieces that combine shelves and cabinets. In the present case, it would appear to be the latter form that is referred to.

119 The wind rose from the west: An echo of the *incipit* of *Manalive* (1912), by G. K. Chesterton: "A wind sprang high in the west . . ."

129 In endeavoring to describe the truly painful events that have occasioned such damage and unrest in the town of Vigàta: Cf. Dostoyevsky, *The Possessed* (1871), which begins: "In undertaking to describe the recent and strange incidents in our town . . ."

138 "Oh, what a beautiful day!": Slight variation on the opening line of the poem *L'è el dì di Mort, alegher!* (1932), by Milanese dialect poet Delio Tessa (1886–1939): "My, what a beautiful day!"

141 *And how are your horns?*: A reference to the fact that the commissioner's wife is cheating on him, making him a cornuto.

142 *tresette . . . briscola*: Italian card games.

146 *And it's a good thing*, **thought Salamone,** *that your horns don't yet reach the chandelier*: See note to p. 141.

148 How much longer is this going to last?: The opening to Arthur Schnitzler's novella *None but the Brave* (*Leutnant Gustl*) (1901).

158 I am an elementary school teacher: The opening to *Il maestro di Vigevano* (1962), a novel by Lucio Mastronardi (1930–1979). The book was made into a film with the same title, by Elio Petri, in 1963.

165 field watcher: In Sicily, major landowners often resorted to the use of private guards, called *campieri*, to protect their lands and crops from bandits. They were also used as strongmen and avengers. As mentioned in the text that follows, it is only the latter purpose to which this man is put in this case.

168 *Fannu tutte accussì* by a certain Mozzat . . . *U flautu magicu:* With a hilarious touch appreciable perhaps only to Italian ears, Camilleri has his character Sicilianize the Italian titles of the Mozart operas *Così Fan Tutte* and *The Magic Flute*, which would be *Il Flauto Magico* in proper Italian.

171 An ordinary-looking young man: An echo of the opening of *The Magic Mountain,* by Thomas Mann: "An unassuming young man . . ." (translated by H. T. Lowe-Porter, 1924).

183 If on a winter's night already: A send-up of the opening line and title of *If on a Winter's Night a Traveler,* by Italo Calvino (1981).

194 *It was a pleasure to set the fire:* A variation on the opening of *Fahrenheit 451* (1953), by Ray Bradbury: "It was a pleasure to burn . . ."

204 *Giagia my dear:* A direct quote of the opening of *Anime e nudo,* a play by Marco Praga (1862–1929).

205 *Aleardi, the poet over whose pages, in the years that followed, we were to weep so many tears, heave so many sighs:* Aleardo Aleardi (1812–1878), a late-Romantic poet of aristocratic birth who was known mostly for his high-blown eloquence in celebration of civic values. One of his more famous pieces is called *Il matrimonio* (1842), which celebrates marriage as civic virtue. It is with tongue firmly in cheek that Camilleri makes Aleardi Prefect Bortuzzi's favorite poet.

213 The oranges were more plentiful than usual that year: A direct quote of the opening of *Clea* (1965), by Lawrence Durrell.

220 "the difference between a common bully and a man of honor": In the common ethos of the "old Mafia," a "man of honor" is indeed a mafioso. But, as the term implies, the mafioso was held to a code of honor that implied, among other things, no harming of women and children, and no arbitrary violence against personal enemies. Violation of this code could lead to elimination by one's peers. Obviously this code is now a thing of the past, though some of the elder members of the current Sicilian Mafia still use the term "man of honor" to mean a member of la Cosa Nostra.

Notes by Stephen Sartarelli